PRAISE FOR *BYE-BYE BAKERSFIELD*

"*Bye-Bye Bakersfield* is both hilarious and heartbreaking. It is a poignant, wickedly sharp coming-of-age tale fueled by the voice of a plucky, spirted protagonist that is unforgettable."

—Suzy Vitello, award-winning author of *The Moment Before*.

"This funny, amazing book is a joy to read. Baross gives us a coming-of-age story that touches on race, religion and politics in a small conservative town. Her narrator, the outsider, must also contend with a mother and her "Rules Written in Stone."

—Steven Allred, award-winning author of *The Alehouse at the End of the World*.

"Baross skillfully weaves hilarity and pathos together into a portrait of a daring young girl rebelling against small town constraints and her heroic leap out of Bakersfield."

—Sallie Kravetz, author/photographer.

BYE-BYE BAKERSFIELD

a novel by

Jan Baross

MPolo Press

Acknowledgement to publications in which these chapters were first published:

"Christmas Shoplifting": First Place-International San Miguel Writers Competition.

"Prom Night": Second Place. Timberline Review.

janbaross.com

First Edition: published 2023

Cover Artwork and Design: Jan Baross

Book Design: Andrew Durkin

Published by MPolo Press in Oregon

DEDICATION

This book is dedicated to my family,
without whom I would have had nothing to write about.

Mothers are as elemental as fire, as you well know.
They burn bright in our lives, whether or not
We've ever suffered their judgement
Or merely been terrified by their love.

The telling of a life tends to falsify, to give it a form it did not intrinsically possess. This is just the fact of writing things down.

JOAN DIDION

INTRODUCTION

With lengthy perspective, I have herded tension, searing humanity and flat-out Jewish humor into a structure of related short stories that is this book.

If you have ever skipped a stone across water, you will understand the trajectory of these related pieces.

This has been hard, grown-up work over decades that resulted in a deeper understanding of loved ones I thought I knew, and have learned since that I did not.

Now that the book of my dead family is complete, I take long dog-walks in the cemetery, look up at the sky, and shout,

"Look, I'm sorry!"

PROLOGUE

Santa Barbara, CA. January 2019

A warm Santa Barbara breeze blew through the screened window of Mother's hotel suite.

Just a few months shy of one-hundred-and-four years old, her eyes still sparked with a bright, competitive glow.

"Gin!" she said, and laid her cards down.

She always beat me with such a single-minded pleasure.

I shuffled the cards for another game and glanced up at her smile.

After thirty years living in London, and these last twenty, basking in the gentle light of Santa Barbara, she looked like a million bucks. Her make-up was perfect. Dressed in a dazzling maroon knit suit, she sat in her comfy green TV chair, and began to add up our scores.

"You know," she said, "At this age I have so much wisdom, and nowhere to put it. Who wants to hear it? Not you. I lead this easy, unfettered life. You could be just like me by simply adhering to my written-in-stone rules. For example. . ."

Any sentence of hers that began with *for example* included not only what I should be doing, but the long list of things I had failed to do. Over many years, I had learned to listen, nod, and smile, as though we were dating.

"For example, if you'd listened to me before you got married," said Mother, "you would have heard me say, don't fall in love, don't marry, and don't have children. It's all an unnatural act."

"As I recall, you wanted me to get married so you could feel unencumbered," I said.

"That too," she said.

Undiminished in mind, but literally on her last legs, she continued.

"When I do die, which I'm beginning to doubt, just follow my flawless example of how to present yourself to the world. Always wear lipstick. Be normal on the outside. Keep your expectations low and you'll keep your blood pressure low. Everything is private, particularly grief. Anything you let out of your control will come back to bite you. Don't ask woo-woo questions like, *Why I am here?* Only drink water when you're on the toilet so you don't waste time."

"That last one actually sounds useful," I said. "Now here's a question for you. Is there an upside to being so old?"

"You bet," she said, brightening. "You no longer give a shit."

I was shocked. "You've never sworn before. Aren't you supposed to set a good example?"

Clearly enjoying her effect, she said, "Jan, you're seventy-six years old. Fuck it!"

"Mother, Jesus!"

She continued. "My exemplary lifestyle includes two hours of sleep a night, never drinking water, and the wisdom to know that exercise is an abomination. My favorite meal is two scoops of pistachio ice cream, a demitasse of espresso, and a chaser of double-thick Ruffles potato chips."

It worked for her. I'd watched this svelte woman rebound like a pro from every major crisis life threw at her. Broken hip, broken ribs, pneumonia, cancer, a deadly flu, the early deaths of her husband from a heart attack and her son from a car accident. After Mother's latest fall in the bathtub even her doctor said, "You should be dead."

"Now *your* birth," said Mother, on a roll, "was like pushing a container of Rocky Road through a pinhole. I, for one, would have gone through childbirth only once to satisfy my curiosity. But if you ask me, I don't recommend it. I endured the second time for your father. Thank God, I gave him a son to carry on the family name."

"Seriously? Meadoff?" I said. It always sounded like flesh falling off a corpse.

"It was Medvedyev. Bear, in Russian," said Mother. "A clerical fool on Ellis Island changed it. And speaking of idiots, you know what nearly killed me after you were born?"

"Something else I get to feel guilty about?" I said.

"The ambulance," said Mother. "Two college boys were driving us home from the hospital. Royal treatment for a doctor's wife. I was on a stretcher, so I asked the one nearest you, 'How's the baby? He looked down and yelled. 'Oh my God, she's stopped breathing! Go back!'

The other idiot makes a crazy U-turn. I remember the word blue. *She's turning blue.* That word still jumps out at me when I hear it in normal conversation. Then the first idiot said: 'Oh, never mind, she's breathing again.' Then the two of them laughed like nut cases. I couldn't get them fired even if I wanted to. The war made every fool indispensable."

"Be grateful," I said. "I'm here. I'm healthy."

"Too healthy!" she said. "Nowadays they'd call you hyperactive. You never crawled like a normal baby. One day you just got up and started running. I'll never forget, you were jumping up and down in the front seat of the car. The door flew open, and you fell out. I had to leap from the moving car, pick you up, and leap back in the car while it was still rolling down the street. At home, you'd run and jump down the stairs and sometimes land on your head. A friend said to me, let her alone and she'll learn to slow down. Another friend said, stop her before she makes herself stupid."

"I'll bet I know which advice you followed," I said.

"I never said you were stupid," said Mother.

CHAPTER 1
THE PROMISED LAND

I had my hat on the whole time.
—Mother

Bakersfield, July 1950

Mother and I protested all the way through the burlap-colored Tehachapi Mountains.

Daddy had uprooted us from the cool breezes of San Francisco Bay and plunged our overheated Chevy into the stifling San Joaquin Valley.

The width of the valley was split by a black spine of highway or the mirage of a highway that wavered in the breathless heat. Ahead of us lay a dry landscape of biblical proportion.

Death by Cossacks had propelled Daddy out of a Russian ghetto. Now his immigrant answer to our survival was to grab the first job offer he could find, which planted our Jew tent in the heart of redneck central, Bakersfield, California, a small outpost of primitive politics, hot flat aggressive agriculture, and a land swollen with oil.

Mother understood what lay ahead. A woman of big-city possibilities, she had endured a Southern childhood, indentured to small-town sensibilities. Now Daddy was returning her to that same insular life. Why hadn't she protested more?

"In those days, you followed your man into whatever insane sunset he chose," she had said.

Today it was Highway 99.

Our Chevy sped along the valley floor past motels clumped like tiny refugee camps behind the palms. The wind was sharp with desert sand and the smell of the highway. An occasional dust-covered eucalyptus drooped a loose welcome, dead leaves spiraling in our wake.

"Don't just sit there, children," said Mother. "Remember those trees. You may never see them again."

Mother's particular road-trip mantra, "You may never see *them* again," always set a terror ticking in me. How could my seven-year-old eyes gather in all those images ghosting past? And was life so brief that I could never retrace my steps to those blurred palms?

I wondered if it was the early death of her father, that formed and deformed within Mother a volcanic impatience not to waste time. She seemed compelled to inhale every breath of data from the universe, as though cramming for an exam.

Drowsy with the heat, little brother and I sighed and maintained our vigil at the window.

Mother snorted as she read a looming billboard: *Fluoride Equals Communism.*

A series of smaller signs appeared along the highway. Mother and Daddy read them together as we passed each one.

The boy who gets
His girl's applause
Must act
Not Look
Like Santa Claus
BURMA SHAVE!

In those days before seatbelts, my boredom was easily relieved by rolling across the back seat for a tired assault on damp little brother. I pinched Tommy's pudgy thigh, taking pleasure in his quiet gasp. The blond prince bit his lip to keep silent, not wanting to get me in trouble. I resented his loyalty almost as much as I resented his birth.

Mother glanced back at our silence; her eyes unfocused. She was so far from her dream of "circumambulating the arrondissements" of Paris. She dreamt in symphonic uplifts; a glass apartment against a Paris sky, the aroma of lathered espresso, steaming crepes served in outdoor cafés where the recent rubble of war had made every cobblestone an upended shrine.

Mother sighed and adjusted the large straw hat that hid her ivory skin from the sun. She would wear that hat whenever she wanted to remind Daddy of his Exodus promise: "We'll only be here one year, Estelle."

Just until he'd gotten a nest egg together that would sustain our flight back to the cool refuge of San Francisco Bay. Over the next quarter-century we'd hear Mother say with growing alarm, and less and less humor: "Daddy, whenever you're ready."

Ahead was a green highway sign that read, *Fun, Sun, Stay, Play. Welcome to Bakersfield. Population: 40,462.*

"Oh God," said Mother. "Are we really here?"

Mother's personal diaspora in the vast Mojave had begun.

I shielded my eyes against the plate-glass glare of store windows. The Nile, a baroque movie house, contrasted with the board-game sameness of the other buildings. The main street was wide enough to sail a royal barge over the wavy asphalt heat.

Daddy drove us slowly through one dried-up neighborhood after another. A dog with a long tongue lay collapsed in the sparse shade. Tumbleweeds were trapped against a cyclone fence. On the corner of a potholed street, Mother checked the address and moaned. Daddy sighed his apology and turned left on Butler Road.

Our steaming engine got us up the short driveway. The roof of the small brick house was covered in red tiles. On the black wooden door, 709 hung like a prison-cell number.

"Who paints a door black?" said Mother.

I was barely alert from the staggering heat. Tommy and I tumbled out of the car that had become a four-wheeled toaster oven. The cement driveway burned through our thin-soled leather sandals. I wanted to rip off my sweaty sunsuit. How could anyone even dress for such a place?

Daddy, a man of endless gratitude, was all smiles. Our very first home. He handed Mother the key. I'm sure he felt she would adapt, that we all would.

To enter, we had to step on a cement block that was not attached to the house.

The sun-dried door swung open easily. Inside the thick walls, it was cool but stuffy. Daddy opened the windows and left the door wide. The four of us stood in the middle of the empty front room. The polished cement floor was painted red as though it had recently been hosed down with an open artery.

The bare walls seemed to deepen our isolation. Mother put her damp hands on our shoulders and drew us close to her, as though we were in danger.

"Children," Mother whispered, "don't tell anyone you're Jewish. No one. Understood?"

We nodded at our fragile inheritance. Tommy and I had been inoculated with our parent's residual Holocaust fear. That horror had ended shortly after I was born. In another time and place, we could have been executed for being the same people who stood in the middle of this crimson floor.

There was a knock at the open door. Startled, we all turned as if attached to the same thought. A postman in a blue cap made a kind of salute with a letter in his hand. His tanned face and arms were covered with deep wrinkles.

"You the new Jewish doc, Doc?" the postman said.

Mother's nails sank into my shoulder. I held my breath. Tommy reached for my hand. His curly blond hair trembled. Daddy said nothing but nodded slightly, trying his gracious best to comply and deny.

The postman stepped up onto the cement block and leaned into the house. Daddy reached out to take the letter.

"Welcome to Bakersfield, folks," said the postman.

He walked back down the driveway, whistling.

Daddy looked at the envelope. Slowly, as though it were foreign to him, he read our name, scoured free of ghetto syllables.

"Meadoff. Does that sound Jewish to you?"

The air out of Mother's lungs was like a punctured tire. She walked to the door, shielding her eyes against the glare of the sun.

"One year, Daddy," she said.

CHAPTER 2
THE HUMAN HEART

Never waste time just eating.
—Mother

Bakersfield, July 1950

Our first day in this new house, even the fan gave up and creaked to a slow stop. Tommy flipped the fan blades with his chewed pencil, but it was no use. You'd need a hammer to stir the air.

The four of us sat at the kitchen table, rubbed ice cubes on our arms, and wiped our faces with washrags that Mother had put in the fridge. We were sucked dry unpacking our San Francisco life into this small desert house.

The only food we had left was dried sandwiches and hard-boiled eggs.

"We've got to get stocked up with some staples," said Mother.

She opened the Yellow Pages Directory and leafed through with a damp finger.

"The A&P and Safeway are all the way across town," she said. "What kind of godforsaken neighborhood is this? They don't believe in franchise?"

"Now, Estelle," said Daddy. He held the cold Coke bottle against his neck. "Didn't we pass a mom-and-pop store a couple blocks over? I'll get the keys."

"I'm not climbing back in that car," said Mother.

She put on her large sun hat, picked up an umbrella and handed me an empty bag. I followed her into the blistering late-afternoon heat. Elbow to elbow, we shuffled forward under the black umbrella's shade.

Butler Road was lumpy and covered in dust. Unlike our sparse digs, the other houses had porches, tall trees, and green watered lawns. One house had a big lawn surrounded by a prison-high cyclone fence. On the other side was a red-haired boy caged with two sheep dogs tearing at a rag doll.

"Hi!" I hollered.

The boy turned away and jumped on one of the dogs for a fight. I'd have to check him out later.

We found the mom-and-pop grocery store in front of an orange grove. I'd never seen a building so close to falling down. Clapboard splintering, roof sagging. The only color was a red neon Schlitz Beer sign in the window. Three letters flickered *B-E-E.*

As we entered, the rusty screen door squeaked and slammed shut behind us. It was cool inside and blinding dark after all that sunlight. When my eyes adjusted, I saw rows and rows of cans. Tuna, beans, dog food. Campbell's soup claimed a whole shelf. Tide and soaps took up another. Near the wall were droopy vegetables in big boxes. The only thing interesting was the wobbly rack of comics.

"You want a *Tarzan*?" said Mother.

The comics were kid-handled and grease-edged, but Tarzan was my man. What I wouldn't give to swing through the trees with him and a bunch of chimp pals.

"We can bear this diet for a couple meals," said Mother, spreading the groceries on the counter; two cans of Campbell's chicken soup, a soft loaf of Langendorf bread, Darigold butter, a gallon of milk, twelve eggs, and Folgers coffee.

The cash register lady was old, short and wore a flowered apron over a pale green dress. One of her eyes was faded and the other was sky-blue. Her smile was so friendly I decided to chat.

"Your beer sign is broken. It only says *bee*," I said.

"That's why everyone calls me Aunt Bee," said the old lady. "Y'all new to the neighborhood. What church you belong to?"

With the steaming soup and no fan, our house was hot as hell. I set out the best bowls, but nothing helped. Not even the food.

The Langendorf bread was like Kleenex. I rolled my slice into a doughy ball the size of a marble and shot it across the table at Tommy. He just dumped it in his salty soup and kept eating.

Mother shoved her half-finished bowl aside and snapped open *Time* magazine.

"Never waste time just eating," she always said. "You kids need this information in preparation for the insane world you're about to inherit."

Since breaking news always went with breaking bread in our house, Tommy and I were never far from Mother's relentless broadening of our minds. She insisted on up-to-date children with firm opinions that matched her own. Tommy and I knew to listen because that was the deal. You could ask us anything about current events and we could line it up for you.

Tonight, Mother's rant centered on Senator Joseph McCarthy and his HUAC committee, who were pulling the country apart by calling everyone a Commie.

"They'll let any nut case in that spineless, do-nothing Congress!" she said.

Stupidity on any level made Mother angry, but her rage never left the kitchen.

"We don't make waves in public," she always said. "Unmade waves are the key to your Jewish survival kit. Keep your heads down. Don't stand out. Never complain. And, if you want friends in this godforsaken town, do not tell people you're a Democrat."

"We can't tell people we're Jewish," I said. "And we can't tell people we're Democrats. What *can* we say that won't make them mad at us?"

"Jews have been asking that question for four thousand years," said Mother.

When she closed *Time* magazine, dinner was over. We washed the dishes and took cold showers, for all the good that did.

I hunkered under the covers in my new bedroom and tried to get comfy, but the silence in this new house was spooky.

In our old San Francisco two-story, the family was always connected by sound; Mother's slipper-flipping tread over creaky wooden floors, Daddy's soft voice through the heat vents, muffled medical bedtime stories he invented just for Tommy.

But here, in this one-story house, our bedrooms were miles apart down a dark hallway. Mine was at this end. The parents were at the other end. Tommy's bedroom was in between.

I heard a loud, high sneeze. Finally, Mother was on her way to my bedroom with a *Reader's Digest* bedtime story.

She slumped against my doorway, bleary-eyed. I wasn't used to seeing her this wiped out. It was like she was imitating someone who was tired.

"I can't find The *Digests*," she said. "Besides, I'm tired after all the unpacking."

"But I need a story," I whined. "You could make up a medical one like Daddy does for Tommy."

Mother cracked her knuckles. "Blood and guts? Not my cup of tea."

"Pleaaase," I said.

"You want medical? Fine," she said. "Once upon a time, you marry a doctor. He supports you. You live happily ever after. The end."

She snapped off the overhead light and disappeared down the dark hallway. I couldn't hear her footsteps. That soft carpet ate everyone's direction.

Who the heck needed *Reader's Digest* anyway. I knew where to find a story. Daddy would be telling Tommy some weird medical adventure. He was only six, but Daddy always said the greatest gift a father could give his son was a profession.

"Hold down the fort, soldier," I said to my giant doll, Johnny. I got him for my seventh birthday. We wore the same size Levi's.

I snapped back the bedspread frills and slid to the carpet. Down the dark hallway, the night felt strange without big-city sounds. No screaming ambulances, motorcycles roaring, or drunks singing on the sidewalk. No sidewalks.

I snooped into Tommy's lit doorway. He was on his bed, leaning back on his pillow like a chubby god. His fat foot rested against Daddy's leg. Those guys were all smiles, looking at each other. No room for anyone else in that picture. I inhaled, filled my lungs like ammunition, and stepped into the room.

"Can I hear too?" I said.

Tommy waved me in with a smile.

"Hey, Sis." I never understood why he was always so glad to see me.

Daddy's dark eyebrows returned from their surprise trip up his forehead.

"No *Reader's Digest*?" he said.

I shook my head and jumped onto the bed between them. They shifted to make room. I sat cross-legged. One knee touching Tommy and one knee touching Daddy.

"Sweetheart," said Daddy, "these are medical stories. There's blood involved."

"I love blood!" I said.

We all knew that wasn't true. I almost puked when Daddy told us about the old drunk who rode boxcars and never changed his socks. The guy's skin had grown over the argyle. Daddy had to cut the material out piece by piece and the cuts were deep enough that there was a lot of blood. He told the drunk that if he didn't change his ways, someday an infection would kill him. The drunk said, "There's more old drunks out here than there are old doctors."

Daddy thought that was one of the best comebacks he'd ever heard.

Mother didn't find it amusing. When Daddy died years later at age 54, I wondered if that old bum was still riding the rails.

Tommy leaned back on his pillow. Daddy cleared his throat. Always the sign of a beginning.

"Once upon a time," he said, "a pterodactyl lands on your front porch. He's been badly wounded in a fight with a tyrannosaurus rex. What do you do to help him?"

"How do I know?" I said. "You're the one telling the story."

"Sweetheart," said Daddy, "I ask questions so you can learn by your answers."

"It's the Socratic method," said Tommy.

"The what?" I said.

"Here's the first clue," said Daddy. "Blood is pulsing out of the pterodactyl's chest."

Simple. I could do this. "He's bleeding to death," I said.

"Pulsing!" said the little genius. "Means an artery's been severed."

"Excellent!" said Daddy. "OK, you two, climb aboard!"

Wait a minute. What just happened? The two of them were sitting on the bed and began rowing fast with invisible paddles like the bed was a boat. This was nuts!

"Row!" Tommy shouted. "We gotta get through the hole in his chest."

"Lend a hand, sweetheart," said Daddy. "We're paddling against the current."

I picked up an invisible oar and rowed too. And rowed. And rowed. I swear I began to feel the blood under us like a giant river. Finally, we got inside. Daddy said my extra muscle really helped. He showed us both how to sew an artery together.

"Would you like to take the last stitch, sweetheart?" said Daddy.

I shook my head. I was feeling a little sick with all that blood.

Downstream was easier. Once we were outside of the pterodactyl, Tommy stitched its leathery skin together and tied a big hero knot.

"Good work, both of you," said Daddy.

He was doing that grown-up thing, being fair even though I hadn't really done anything.

Tommy went from grinning to grabbing his chest in pain.

"Ow! Ouch! Oh, help, I'm having a heart attack!"

He flopped back on the pillow, his eyes rolling.

Daddy pushed up and down gently on Tommy's chest. He picked up the old stethoscope he'd given Tommy and listened to his heart. They both looked so serious I wanted to cry.

Daddy put the stethoscope in Tommy's ears so he could listen to his own heart.

He gave a nod to Daddy. "The patient will live." He dangled the stethoscope in front of me. "Here, Sis. You wanna have a heart attack?"

I shook my head. What I wanted was to kill them both.

Tommy sat up and said to Daddy, "My fee, or I can bill you."

Daddy gave him a real nickel. Tommy was earning a living? And I got what? *Reader's Digest*? Daddy offered me a nickel too.

"No. I didn't earn it, so that's OK," I said, and I slid off the bed. "Good night, you guys."

The hallway seemed longer on my way back.

I climbed up under the frilly bedspread and cuddled with my Johnny doll.

I couldn't win with Tommy around. One of the only times I got Daddy to myself, he showed me how to draw Greek columns. Doric, Ionic, Corinthian. He said he wanted to be an architect when he was young, but now I was the family artist. Sure, but compared to Tommy, I was still chopped liver.

I socked Johnny doll in the gut until I was tired, but that didn't help.

The next morning, I tried to figure out how to feel better. Maybe I could catch up to Tommy by looking at Daddy's medical books. They were still packed in boxes. I couldn't read them, but they had lots of pictures.

The first book I opened nearly made me puke. One page after another of skin diseases. Unbelievable stuff. I kept turning the pages to see how much I could take, like walking barefoot on hot asphalt. Then I saw a black-and-white photo of a man in front of a palm hut. I tried sounding out the words above his picture: *Elephantiasis of the genitalia.* His penis and balls were so big, they laid on a flat wooden wheelbarrow in front of him so he could walk. The poor guy. How could he pee? Did he have any friends? Where would they sit?

I had to show this picture to Tommy. It was perfect. I mean, he was so kind and sympathetic, I could just see him bursting into tears, gagging, running away, and abandoning the medical profession. Then Daddy would have to hand the family stethoscope to me. Being a doctor was last thing I wanted to do. But that wasn't the point. I just needed to try.

When I walked into Tommy's room, he smiled like always. But this time he held up a bright red-and-blue plastic toy.

"Look what I put together, Sis!" he said. "A human heart. Auricle, ventricle, superior and inferior vena cava."

If we were superior and inferior vena cavas, there's no question which one the little genius would be. He was so happy sharing that I started to regret what I was about to do.

"Ever seen this before?" I said, setting the book on his desk.

I waited for him to turn pale, scream in horror, run out of the room. But he just kept staring at the picture.

"Hey Sis," he said. "How much bigger could his penis get, do you think, before it exploded?"

I was stunned at how wrong this was going. As Tommy examined the picture, he seemed more and more like Daddy. Why did I think I could be better than him? This kid could stitch the spouting artery of a pterodactyl, survive nightly heart attacks, construct a human heart, and not be repulsed by a penis the size of an airplane hangar.

I got so mad. I grabbed the book away from him and smashed it on the heart. Red and blue plastic pieces scattered like insects across the desk. It felt good, but only for a second.

Tommy never cried, even when he should. Instead, he got down on his knees and picked up the pieces. I felt like kicking myself in the face for what I'd done.

"I'm sorry," I said.

I got down on my knees and handed him the broken parts. "I don't know why I did that."

Tommy looked at me.

"I know why," he said. "Daddy loves me better. Don't feel bad, Sis. Mommy loves you best. I get sad too."

I was breathless. Tommy pretty much summed up how things worked with the family. He was a whole year younger than me, but so much smarter.

"Why can't you just be a little kid?" I said.

"Because I'm a grown-up inside," said Tommy.

Mother walked in on us picking up the broken pieces and, when she asked, I told her what had happened.

"This jealousy has got to stop!" she said. "Your little brother is yours to protect. No more violence! And no more cowboy movies for a month."

I was grounded in my room and played solitaire so I could finally win at something.

I couldn't see or hear Daddy and Tommy. But I could feel them down the hall. The two of them sitting side by side, repairing the human heart.

CHAPTER 3
ON TOP OF OLD BALDY

The kids may tease you for a day or two, but then they'll stop.
—Mother

Bakersfield, September 1950

"Don't hurt her," said little brother. He tapped his knee nervously.

I sat rigid on the kitchen chair.

Mother had a good grip on my ponytail.

I closed my eyes. There was a tug as her scissors chewed slowly through my hair. Finally, she let go. The familiar weight was gone. I turned my head from side to side and missed the soft swish against my neck.

Mother stuffed my dark ponytail in a large manila envelope and sealed it. On the front she wrote *Dye hair this color when you turn gray. Love, Mommy.*

"This'll be in the safe-deposit box when the time comes," she said.

Mother continued cutting. Hunks fell on my eyelashes, cheeks, and the terry-cloth towel around my shoulders.

"How much longer?" I said. "I only have one head."

Would the neighborhood kids even recognize me?

Tomorrow would be my first day of school. And I was going to be the only bald first grader in the history of the world. I kept the tears back. It wasn't easy.

Mother put her scissors down on the kitchen table and picked up Daddy's Remington electric shaver. The hum filled the kitchen. That vibration went right through my eyeballs and loosened the tears. Mother shaved my head front to back, side to side until no more hair fell on my shoulders. Her breath was warm on my scalp.

I wanted to hate her for this, but it was my fault. Mary Ellen and I had been fighting a brutal Siberian winter in her backyard. Wolves lunged at our flip-flops. Their fangs tore our swimsuits to shreds. We covered ourselves in ketchup blood. For a joke, I put her cat Peaches on my head, pulled his feet around my chin. Like *brr.*

Who knew cats could give you a skin disease?

"One last thing," said Mother.

She drew the curtains, shut out the setting sun, and flicked off the overheads. She came at me with a small UV light that turned her face purple and her teeth and eyeballs yellow.

Tommy's yellow smile moved closer to inspect the operation. His breath smelled like Froot Loops.

"Does that light kill the ringworms?" he said.

"They only call it *ringworm*," said Mother. "The UV lights up the fungus so I can see where to put the salve. That's what kills them."

Ringworm. Tinea Capitis. Latin for I'm so screwed.

She glopped cold goo on my scalp with a Q-Tip. I pictured little ringworms gasping for breath, eyes rolling back in their heads. A rain of tiny carcasses bouncing off my T-shirt.

"Mission accomplished," said Mother. "Turn on the lights."

Tommy switched on the kitchen overhead and did a horror-movie gasp.

Holy crap! How bad was it? I raced down the hallway to the bathroom mirror. Jesus! I looked like Daddy's passport photo from Russia.

A kid with his head shaved free of lice. Ears sticking out. *Steerage.* That's what he called that photo of himself.

But I also had yellow salve splotches on my skull, like a circus freak.

"I'm Frankenstein!" I cried.

"Let's put this on you," said Mother, "to protect the furniture."

She came into the bathroom and stretched a thick white cotton cap over my baldness. Now I looked like a mental patient.

"Your hair will grow back in a month or so," she said.

I ran to my bedroom, slammed the door, and flipped on a Nat King Cole record so I could cry.

Mother came in without knocking, and turned down the sound.

"You've really been a sport," she said. "Look what I got you for a reward."

She handed me a small fancy box with a label from her friend, Dori Derry Berry's Shop.

I lifted the lid and found a scarf, soft and glowing. A swish of orange and yellow flowers, no stems. I'd seen the same scarves on the thin shoulders of Mother's Bakersfield bridge club.

"Honest-to-god silk for your first day of school," she said. "It'll cover your cap."

"Kids don't wear scarves!" I said. "I can't go to school looking like that!"

"But it's gorgeous and expensive," said Mother. "Listen, the kids may tease you for a day or two, but then it'll stop."

What she didn't know about kids, it could fill a garage.

All through the night I heard my humiliation train chugging closer and closer. I didn't sleep because I was praying for a high fever. Tomorrow was going to be the worst day of my life. It didn't take much to imagine the stares, the laughs, the nicknames they'd invent.

I was groggy when Mother shouted her usual. "Rise and shine, morning glory!"

I couldn't eat breakfast. The curled bacon reminded me of the slimy ringworms on my scalp. I was still in a nightmare fog when Mother tied the scarf at the nape of my neck. She told me I looked exotic. What I looked like was an old peasant lady. One of those sepia sourpusses in Daddy's old photos.

At the front door, she slipped a note for the teacher into my new John Wayne lunchbox. I could sure use his six-shooter on a day like this.

"I hope it isn't tuna," I said.

"So, eat the apple," said Mother.

Tommy wrapped his chubby arms around me. "Wish I was old enough to go to school," he said. "I'd protect you."

I hugged him back even harder. We both knew what I was in for.

Mother stood at the door.

"Someday you'll look back on all this and laugh," she said.

A lot of good that was going to do me today!

I ran to join up with Elmer and the neighborhood gang trooping past. I was ready to take on anyone who made fun of me, but no one said anything. Elmer was spending his meanness on a new kid, a boy with dark blue skin. Just walking made the kid breathe hard, like he wasn't getting enough air.

"Hey, blue boy!" said Elmer.

"Piss off, lardo!" gasped blue boy.

Say, he was no slouch, even if he was nearly purple.

At the end of Butler, we looked both ways and crossed the street fast. We ran up the canal levee to where the dirt path stretched a dusty half mile to Castro Lane Grammar School. A soft morning breeze spread DDT fumes. There'd been another mosquito spray on the canal. I wiped my nose on my sleeve. We kicked at the piles of dead grasshoppers laying in a mess of orange weeds. Mosquitos had a weird disease that made your brain swell up. I asked Daddy if I got a bigger brain would it make me smarter? He said no.

The other kids ran ahead. I was in no hurry to get to school. I slid down the slope to the edge of the canal's slow current. It was so much cooler and not as smelly. I could see crawdads slinking in and out of their muddy caves. In the weeds, somebody had left a safety pin fishline with a small weight. I dropped it into the oily water and broke up my ugly reflection. Right away there was a taker. I pulled up a baby crawdad and pried him off the safety pin. His pinchers were opening and closing.

He was crazy to clamp. Some kids put the big crawdads on their nose and let them pinch until blood ran out of their nostrils.

I lifted the little guy so he could see past the suburbs.

"There's a whole world out there, kiddo," I said.

Panic revved the critter's little side-legs. I dropped him back into the water and watched him sink.

"Someday you'll look back on all this and laugh," I said.

From the sun, I could tell it was getting late. The weeds were heating up and the DDT fumes stunk worse. I trotted along the path as fast as I could toward school.

The bell must've rung because the only things moving in the schoolyard were the swings on long chains, stirred by tiny dust devils. A playground without kids had kind of an empty smell.

The classroom door was open to catch a cool morning breeze. I brushed canal mud off my Mary Janes thinking how to ease inside. I tugged the flower scarf forward to my eyebrows, hoping it covered the yellow-stained stocking cap. After a deep breath, I stepped into the classroom. It smelled like disinfectant, chalk dust, and tuna sandwiches.

"Who's this tardy!" said the teacher. "Come forward!"

I walked toward her holding out Mother's note. Kid snickers got loud.

The teacher's pencil eyebrows shot up as she read the note. She started to touch my shoulder. Then she took her hand back and said to turn around and face the class.

"Children," she said. "You may wonder why your little classmate is wearing this lovely scarf." She paused so everyone would pay attention. "Your young friend has ringworm. It's very contagious. If you touch her, you'll have to have your head shaved too."

The whole room went, "Yeeeew!"

The teacher held up her hand for silence.

"Take your seat at the back, young lady," she said. "As I was saying, children, welcome. I am Miss Joseph."

I headed down the aisle. Everyone scooted sideways so nothing on me touched nothing on them. Even my friend Elmer scooted away. His lips were tight over his teeth. I walked close and brushed his elbow on purpose. He squealed.

"Fercrissakes, it's just me!" I said.

"Language!" said Miss Joseph.

I slumped into the last desk of the row and stowed my John Wayne lunchbox under the seat.

Miss Joseph put Mother's note on her desk and pulled down a big map.

"Now children, eyes on California," she said. "Does anyone know why we're called Bakersfield?"

Who in their right mind would put up their hand? No one did.

"Well, children, once upon a time, in 1869, Mr. Thomas Baker had a field along the Kern River. Folks came to find gold in the Kern River and pretty soon there was a town. Mr. Baker decided to name the town after himself, so today we're called Bakersfield."

Boy, there's a guy with no imagination. If I had to name this town, I'd call it Dead Grasshopper Gulch or Backwater Butthole.

Maybe it was Miss Joseph's dull voice, but most of the kids sunk down in their seats. I couldn't listen to anymore history either. I looked out the window and saw a tan horse in a backyard stable behind someone's house. His big ding-dong was sticking out, and he was trying to reach the mares on the other side of the barbed wire. I opened my notebook and drew him. Manes, tails, and ding-dongs were easy. Hooves were the hardest. Time must have gone by pretty fast because the recess bell rang before I'd finished.

"Children," said Miss Joseph, "when you return, we are going to practice duck and cover. Does anyone know what that is?"

"Something to do with ducks?" said Elmer.

"No, dear. It has to do with the A-bomb," said Miss Joseph. "You're excused."

Kids busted out of the room like hornets from a broken nest.

I kept drawing, head down. I knew what was waiting outside.

"You have to go exercise, dear," said Miss Joseph. "It's the law."

I folded the drawing four times so no one could see it and slipped it into my notebook. I got up slowly and put my feet into a square of linoleum next to my desk. Then, one square at a time, I stepped toward the door, trying to take up all of recess. Miss Joseph's chalky fingers tapped her desk.

"Move along, dear," she said.

I stopped at the door and looked out. The cement walkway was jammed with yelling kids, big and small, all the grades, churning around like a bowl full of Cheerios.

I could feel sweat on my upper lip.

"Go!" said Miss Joseph.

I breathed deep and stepped outside. Some kids stopped and looked at me.

"Hey, Granny!" That voice drowned out all the others. "Come here!"

It was Cal. Cal the Giant.

Everyone in our neighborhood knew to stay blocks away from him. Square shoulders, square head, greasy blond hair. He was a sixth grader for the second time. Cal smoked real cigarettes, not dried backyard weeds like the rest of us. He knew grown-up stuff like why dogs got stuck together. If Cal pulled off the scarf, I'd never live down my ugly.

"Come here, you old biddy!" Cal yelled. His buddies laughed.

I turned and ran past girls playing jacks on the walkway, past boys shooting marbles in the dirt. A red rover game almost tripped me up. But I made it to the wide-open playground and ran straight through a dodge ball game. I thought of climbing to the top of the jungle gym where kids were leaping off into the sand. But one of the swings was free so I jumped on, back-stepped as far as I could, and swung my legs straight out. Back and forth, pumping hard.

Cal and his three buttheads strutted up slow.

No need for them to hurry. I'd pretty much trapped myself.

They stood in front of the swing trying to look up my skirt. Cal jumped up and made a grab for my Mary Janes.

I kicked at his head. He hollered swear words.

Kids gathered and looked up like I was a drive-in movie. From up here everyone looked like a stranger. Even Elmer. I pumped hard. My legs were cramping. I kept pumping.

Finally, the bell rang.

Kids peeled off and trotted back to class.

"I'll get ya, Miss Ugly!" Cal yelled and loped off with his gang.

That stung. Because even without the scarf, no one ever said I was pretty. Well, Grandma. But everyone knows about Grandmas.

My feet scraped the ground to a stop. Palms sweaty. I wanted to sneak home. But there was tomorrow and tomorrow, and it seemed long enough to be forever, so I might as well face it now. I gimped back to class, legs shaking. When I came in, Miss Joseph pointed her ruler at me.

"You'll write *I will not be tardy* in your notebook a hundred times," she said.

I sat at my desk and pressed the pencil tip so hard it went through two sheets of paper. All those *I will not be tardy* gave me a red blister on my finger. At least I didn't have to duck under my desk like the rest of the class each time Miss Joseph yelled, "A-Bomb!"

Finally, the lunch bell rang.

What I handed in was a pretty torn-up piece of punishment.

In the cafeteria, I sat alone, hiding as best I could, behind my John Wayne lunchbox. I knew Cal would be on the lookout. There weren't a lot of lunch-pail kids like me, but Mother didn't want me eating crappy cafeteria food. I ignored the tuna sandwich and bit into the apple.

Elmer walked right by me with his "PPP." Potty poop on a plate. That's what he said his cousin called the cafeteria food. The peanut butter roll did look like a light-brown turd.

Then I saw Cal and his dud-heads walking toward me.

I kept chomping the apple, but I was scanning for the cafeteria monitor, who was supposed to keep us from food fights. Cal came up and bumped his big thigh against the table.

"OK, Granny, take it off."

He said it loud enough so kids at the other tables turned around to see what was going on.

Cal swooped in and grabbed my arm. The apple flew out of my hand. He pulled me toward him across the table and reached for the scarf.

I twisted hard, pulled my arm free, and fell back into the chair. The back of my head hit the wall. Boy, was I in big trouble. I kept the tears inside with a deep breath.

Cal came at me again. What would John Wayne do? I stood up quick and hollered. "Stampede!"

Cal blinked his flat eyes. Then he started for me again.

"You want this?" I said.

I lifted the scarfy mess off my head and held it high like a trophy scalp.

Cal froze. I couldn't believe it. Ugly was a super-power!

"Come and get it!" I said and pointed my scarf at him like a six-shooter.

I stepped toward him, just to see what would happen.

Cal's gang backed away, but he stood his ground. A big tough sixth grader couldn't retreat from a first grader. He couldn't move an inch and keep his glory.

"In-fec-tious," I hissed at Cal, holding the stained bundle out front.

One more step. One more. His nose was going to feel my disease. Just before I gooped him, he jerked his head away. That counted!

I took another step toward him. He had to back up.

One kid hooted, "Go, Baldy!" and started pounding his metal tray with a fork.

Then everyone started fork-pounding.

Cal's thick head turned. He saw the laughing faces.

Cal did this gorilla kick, and an empty chair went flying. But the forks just got louder.

He stalked out of the cafeteria flipping birds with both hands.

Tears forced their way up in my eyes. I snorted it all back inside.

It took me a second to realize. I had just John-Wayned the biggest creep in the school. No one was going to mess with me now. I dropped the scarfy heap on the table.

Some of the grinning kids waved me over. I grabbed my John Wayne lunchbox and sat with them, but not close enough to infect anyone. Even Elmer moved his tray to where I was.

Wow, I thought. *For a baldy, the first day of school couldn't have gone better.*

I saw Miss Joseph striding towards me, roaring through her megaphone.

"STUDENTS! Get away from her! She's diseased!"

I stood up fast and my chair fell over.

"You put that scarf back on, young lady!" said Miss Joseph.

She was breathing hard from her sprint.

"You're suspended for endangering the other children! I'm going to speak to your mother!"

~

On the walk back along the levee, I kicked through piles of dead grasshoppers. It was too early to go home and get in trouble.

I hunkered at the canal's edge.

In the sun, the scarf got so hot, I took it off again. Without thinking much about it, almost like a dream, I leaned over and dropped the flowery silk in the current, watching it spread over my little crawdad's world.

CHAPTER 4
THE CONVERT

Religion will be the death of us all.
—Mother

Bakersfield, August 1952

Mother gathered the family together in the front room. She looked wet-eyed and undone, like she'd been crying in the wind.

Daddy's gaze was focused on the floor.

Tommy and I plopped on the couch and faced our parents.

"As you know, kids," said Mother, wiping her eyes, "I'd rather be dead than spend another minute in this godforsaken town."

No secret there. Daddy had promised us one year in Bakersfield. Then we'd return to San Francisco. It had been two years.

Daddy cleared his throat. "I'm sorry, kids. I haven't been able to save a cent working at the hospital. The only way I can make enough money to set up a practice in San Francisco is if I go into private practice here, just for a couple more years."

Mother sighed and got up. She picked up her cigarettes and went into the back yard for a quiet smoke.

~

A month later, Daddy drove us to his new office. On the dark door was a coppery plaque that glowed in the noonday sun. It read:

Orthopedic Surgeon. And below: *Dr. Nathan Meadoff.*

"A door with a dream," said Daddy softly. I wanted to hug him.

His office was one of about ten small offices built around a big Spanish-style fountain. It was almost downtown and had good parking, so we were supposed to be thrilled about the location.

Tommy and I carried Daddy's books into his new office. Inside the waiting room was a desk, a typewriter, a phone, a filing cabinet, a bookshelf, and three Naugahyde chairs for patients. Down a short hall was a bathroom and a small exam room.

To give the waiting room a homier look, Mother was hanging three black-and-white etchings of boats by an actor named Lionel Barrymore. A pharmacy company sent them every Christmas. We had so many that Daddy let me color in a few.

Mother set her brown purse on top of the desk. She dropped into the chair and twirled in a circle like a dreidel. Her dream of getting out of Bakersfield was dead for now. Even at the tender age of eight, this was a clear lesson to me about marriage, sacrifice, and duty. To be avoided at all costs.

"Welcome to Daddy's chop shop," she said. "Mommy's back to being a working girl."

Her playfulness let us all breathe again. She was going to be a sport about this, since Daddy couldn't afford someone who wasn't Mother. I wondered how long she would last behind a boring desk all day.

"If you could have any job in the world," I said, "what would it be?"

"Research librarian," she said. "Minimal interaction with people. Digging deep into knowledge. Always learning something new. That's my cup of tea."

“Why didn’t you do that?” I said.

She sighed. “Expectations of the times, I suppose. My cousins all got social work degrees so I did too. We pictured ourselves carrying baskets of food to the poor. But my first assignment was to persuade a man on welfare to help support his disabled parents. He got so angry at my *meddling* that he picked up a knife and chased me out of his house, screaming that he would slit my throat if I came back. I jumped in the car and barely escaped.”

“Wow,” I said. “Like *Dragnet*. So, won’t you go nuts sitting in an office all day with no one trying to kill you?”

“Have you ever heard me complain?” said Mother.

“You complain about me all the time,” I said.

“That’s different,” she said.

She looked over at Daddy, and just for a second, her eyes got soft. “Besides, look at your father’s face.”

He was hanging his medical degree on the wall. Yep, that was Daddy’s happy face.

Mother breathed a deep sigh, whipped off the typewriter cover, and started organizing her desk.

In the morning, before Daddy left for the office, Mother straightened his tie, checked his eyes for sleep, and made sure his breath was OK. She’d hadn’t cooked with onions and garlic, so he passed muster.

After he’d gone, she sat down at the breakfast table and wrote an ad for the newspaper.

“We have to find someone to take up the domestic slack around here,” said Mother. “I want a clean Swede. They’re an efficient, antiseptic breed.”

Mother had a thing about germs. She used to boil my toys if I dropped them out of the playpen. I learned to test for temperature. A doctor named Spock had rules about keeping babies sterile.

“If I’d been truly efficient,” Mother joked, “I would’ve boiled the kid.”

The Swedish maid that walked into our lives was Lena, a gaunt, middle-aged woman with black hair and tanned skin toughened by an Arkansas sun. She was dressed in a starched cotton dress that was so faded the flowers were almost gone. Black eyes gawked out from under a deep brow. Her face was so boney I was almost afraid to see what her smile would look like when she got around to it.

Mother said she was the most un-Swedish looking person she'd ever met.

Lena moved into the laundry room with the washer and dryer, stuck her worn suitcase under the twin bed and was home. The bed was where she sorted our laundry. She never used it to sleep. She said that she liked the born-again comfort of a linoleum floor.

It took us a while to get used to her ways. For meals, she'd stuff our leftovers in small glass jars and eat them later with ketchup. It seemed like she was grateful for everything that came her way because she was always saying, "Thank you, Jesus."

And then there was her hymn humming.

Mother always said, "Religion is the most divisive institution created by man and it will be the death of us all."

But she didn't seem to care what Lena did, as long as she kept me and Tommy alive until dinner.

I figured Lena for a pushover because her entire conversation with Mother was, "Yes, Ma'am."

Then one day, after Daddy and Mother left for work, Lena stopped hymn humming and leaned on her mop handle. I ignored her stare and slurped my Cheerios. Summer was yellowing up on the other side of the screen door, so there was a dead-grass promise of a cowboy-and-Indian day. I loved dying full of arrows. Also, my tumbleweed fort needed another layer. Once I got the tumbleweeds piled five deep, no one could get to me.

Lena shuffled closer to the kitchen table with her soap-sud smell.

"Y'all a Christian family?" Lena said in a soft drawl.

My stomach clenched.

Tommy and I looked at each other.

We'd promised Mother to keep our Jew thing secret.

I shrugged at Lena, so I wouldn't give us away.

She must've taken it wrong, because she said, "How'd you children like a Bible story?"

I shrugged again.

"Good. Wait here," she said.

Tommy and I edged for a screen-door getaway. But she came back too fast with a black book in her hand and sat at the head of the table.

"That's Daddy's chair," I said.

In the hard morning light, her skin looked like cracked mud.

"Is this a ghost story?" whispered Tommy.

Lena folded her hands on the black book. "Let us pray."

I knew this game. I folded my fingers together.

"Here's the church." I said, "Here's the steeple. Open the door." I turned my fingers inside out. "And here's all the people."

Tommy giggled. He always got such a kick out of me.

Lena's eyes sunk deeper. "Are you a Christian family?"

Why was she asking us these questions? And sitting in Daddy's chair? She could be fired!

"We're Jews!" I said, "OK?"

Tommy wide-eyed me. Yes, I'd broken our promise to Mother.

Lena's teeth spread yellow in the sunlight. She was smiling.

"Bless my everlasting," she said. She put her hand on her heart. "I dwell among God's Chosen. Someday, children, you and I will abide together in Heaven, when Jesus has cleansed your filthy souls."

"My filthy what?" I said.

"Your spirit, child," said Lena. "He will cleanse your spirit. Then all of us who have been saved will dwell together in the Rapture."

"What's the Rapture?" asked Tommy. "Is that like Knott's Berry Farm? Do they have rides?"

"Heavens, children." Lena stared at us. "Come here."

We got up and stood on either side of her. This close I could smell the starch in her dress. I just wanted to go outside and play. But Lena opened her black book and held it so we could see a picture glued to the inside cover. It was a man nailed to a cross wearing a thorn crown. Blood dripped from wounds on his head and hands and feet. He was nearly naked and had long hair like a girl. But also a beard, which was confusing.

"Who killed the guy?" I said.

Lena seemed surprised. "Why, *you* did, child," she said. "It was you Jews who nailed Jesus to the cross. It is your eternal sin, sweetheart."

"No one in my family would do that!" I said.

Tommy squinted at the picture. "Is he nailed through his tendons or muscle?"

"Can we be excused?" I said.

Lena was really crapping up our morning. Besides, Mother would not want us looking at a nearly naked man.

"Children," said Lena. "Listen to me. Once upon a time, in the land of the Pharaohs, a giant Philistine named Goliath fought a small shepherd boy. The giant was nine feet tall. The boy was a little older than you and his name was David."

OK. I had a short cousin named David so that gave me a picture.

"Goliath's head was wider than the night sky," she said. "His hair was filled with poison snakes."

Poison snakes! My imagination lit up. Lena raised her hands in the air and began swaying.

"Raise your hands children." She moved her arms like tree branches in a storm. "Say *Hallelujah!*"

We raised our hands. "Hallelujah!" Swaying was a great way to tell a story.

Lena started sing-songing her words. "Here comes the giant. Here he comes. 'Little David,' sayeth the Lord, 'Little David, I am your slingshot. I am your stone. Cast me at evil. And evil will die! Hallelujah!' And David slung the stone. It cracked the giant's head and he died. Little David was a hero. But it was Jesus who aimed that deadly stone. Thank you, Jesus."

Lena looked up at our ceiling.

"Praise be, Lord! Save this Jew child!"

Her big hand shot out and covered my face. I nearly fell over, but she held me by the neck with her other hand. Her palm on my face was rough and smelled like soap. I pulled at her fingers for air. I couldn't see. I couldn't breathe.

"Save her, Jesus," sung Lena. "Say it, child!"

My lungs felt hot. I fought her blind. I needed air.

"Say it!" said Lena.

I tasted salt. A red darkness. Was that a face? I stopped fighting.

"Save me, Jesus!" I slobbered into her palm.

Lena let go. I opened my eyes and inhaled deep gulps of air.

"Rejoice, child," said Lena, softly. "Jesus heard your prayer."

She palmed some of her soapy bucket water and dripped it on my head.

"You been cleansed and born again, sugah," said Lena. "Y'all a Christian now."

Water dripped from my hair onto my lips. "Really? So fast?" I spit the soapy drops into the bucket.

Tommy came close and whispered, "I'm pretty sure you're still a Jew."

I felt beat up, but somehow lighter. Lena put her book away and started mopping up. She hymn-hummed like nothing had happened.

"Let's get outta here," said Tommy and ran for the screen door.

I followed him into the back yard, under the blue sky of Jesus. I sat on the swing to sun-dry my hair.

I was so relieved to be a Christian. It was kind of like getting a polio shot, only against another Holocaust. Now I didn't have to hide who I was. If the Nazis came again, I wouldn't get burned up in the ovens. I could count on being alive for the rest of my life. I wondered if Mother would let me keep Jesus. She hated it when I brought home strays.

"Hey," I said to Tommy. "If it's this easy to be a Christian, why don't all the Jews get saved? Then we could rest easy, and Daddy could play golf at the country club."

"Better take that up with Mother," said Tommy.

Being a Christian, I felt superior. So, at dinnertime, I looked Mother in the eye and revealed my plan for the family.

"Lena could save us a lot of trouble," I said, finally.

Mother stood over me with oven-mitten hands on her hips. I heard the steaks start to sizzle under the red-hot coils.

"Listen, to me, young lady," she said. "You can convert to anything want, but you'll always be a Jew in the eyes of the world. You know what happened eight years ago?"

"Sure," I said. "The Holocaust."

I'd seen the newsreels. Kids my age, but hollow-eyed in striped pajamas. Six million of us dead.

"You will never, ever escape your Jewish blood," said Mother. "Just be proud of our resilience, if nothing else."

Mother said that there would be no more converting, but she didn't fire Lena. She said controversy should start at home. That way she could nip it in the bud.

"I'm sending you to Hebrew school for a crash course," said Mother.

That class cleaned the Christian right out of me. I was back to being filled up with the blood that Mother said I could never escape.

What I learned at Hebrew school was that Lena's Bible stories were written by Jews. So, even though the world wanted us dead, they still liked our stories. That was some kind of good news.

Also, I learned that Jesus was a Jew like me. For all the good it did him.

CHAPTER 5
A REAL COWBOY

You *are* West, dumb kid!
—*Mother*

Bakersfield, November 1953

Oilwells cast early morning shadows as Mother's Chevy sped along the highway. I took aim with my finger and pretended to blow one rig apart just as we made a quick right at Fosters Freeze.

We were in real country now. Rutted roads, sagging porches, herds of old cars in tall grass. I was so used to our tidy lawn that clutter like this was an outlaw thrill.

Tommy handed me my fair share of sugar cubes. I'd gotten a whole year of Sunday riding lessons for my tenth birthday. All I dreamt about anymore was spending my life riding the range like a real cowboy.

I shouted to Mother in the front seat. "Soon as I'm grown up, I'm headed West, you know."

Mother laughed. "You *are* West, dumb kid. It's three hours to the Pacific."

"Oh, yeah?" I said.

I hated it when Mother got her facts wrong. I knew there was another West. I'd seen all the matinees. The town with a dusty main street. Guys in black hats up to no good. My hero, John Wayne, saving the day.

Mother braked at the wooden gate. *Irma's Stables* was nearly worn off the cardboard sign. I jumped out of the car. Couldn't hardly wait for the smell of something four-legged. Once I got into cowboy land, I was John Wayne.

Mother shouted, "Wait for your little brother!"

Tommy had been getting clingy lately, and it was driving me nuts. I lifted the gate chain and got him inside the fence. Mother waved and turned her car around to go home.

With Tommy locked in cowboy land, I ran on ahead and left him huffing along the path behind me. Around a bend of high brush, the space opened up. Morning sun heated the red barn roof. Steam rose off like it was a big coffee pot. Next to the barn was the tack room and inside were saddles, reins, stirrups and the good strong smell of horse-blanket sweat.

Irma's rooster, Henry, crowed at me as I ran past. He fluttered onto Irma's big cooler next to her trailer. After the ride it was Cokes all around.

Irma had our horses waiting in the practice ring. That manure stink went straight to my heart. Irma nodded her beat-up Stetson in time to Hank Williams on the dinged-up battery radio. Her skinny bowed legs were under a body round as a Passover roast.

"Hello," I said, but she just took the ride money. I wondered if she even knew my name.

"Hey, Ranger," I said, and stroked his long nose. "Miss me, boy?"

His brown Palomino eyes sunk my heart. Eyelashes thicker than Marilyn Monroe.

I flat-palmed him sugar cubes and got tingles from his soft wide lips. I put my ear against his jaw and heard his huge teeth make a delicious crunch. He had hooves five times bigger than my boots. It felt giant just being near him.

Irma cupped her hands and hoisted me into the saddle. I could see the top of her stained Stetson and a whole lot further. Up this high it was easy to dream like a hero. But looking straight down at the ground made the world spin. Daddy said I had *vertigo*, which sounded a lot like a board game.

Tommy got strapped onto Buster's saddle with a leather belt. His new blue sneakers swam in the worn stirrups, but he was as safe as being in bed. His horse was half the size of Ranger and slow as drool.

Irma climbed on her horse, Cesar, and we followed them out of the practice ring. Cesar pulled on his bit, but Irma got him settled down with her riding crop. Her red-eyed Arabian was so bad-tempered no one could ride him but Miss Iron Legs herself. She tightened the greasy Stetson with its leather strap and pulled her skinny bowed legs tight against the horse's ribs. I'd seen her guide Cesar from knee pressure alone. Here was the woman I wanted to be. Except for the old and ugly.

We threaded through the eye of the narrow trailhead. Madrone trees on either side were a red column entryway into cowboy land. My butt was already synched to the rhythm of Ranger. I looked back for Tommy. He grinned and held onto Buster's saddle horn. His old pony was already breathing heavy behind us.

When the trail widened up, Irma kicked Cesar and bolted off along the Kern River.

"Yee-ha!" she yelled.

She always set a pace on the safe side of dangerous. She didn't rein us in like a normal grown-up.

"Yee-ha!" I yelled.

Ranger sprung into a gallop. Hooves pounding, his great body under my legs. Ranger and me galloping past the cottonwood and giant willows, the wind in our faces and the sun on our backs, riding to save the town—headed for glory, faster and faster, and the bad guys never get us.

We were gaining on Irma's flat butt. The path got wide enough for two horses. This was the first time Irma let us pull up neck and neck, like I was her sidekick! Her deputy! There was nothing we couldn't save!

Then she tore on ahead like she'd been holding back. I felt the cheat of that.

Irma finally reined in under the cottonwoods to let me and Tommy catch up. I stopped beside her, stroked Ranger's neck, and got a swampy handful of sweat. I wiped it on my Levi's.

I'd been riding for months now and hadn't fallen off yet. I felt pretty bad about that.

Irma always told us, "You ain't a real cowboy 'til you fall off, 'cause getting back on is the measure."

She never made conversation on the trail, but I had to ask.

"Irma, even if I never fall off, can I be a real cowboy?" I said.

Irma stretched her mouth, showing her missing side teeth. I was pretty sure it was a grin.

"Some don't never fall off," she said. "They got too much rodeo in 'em."

Even when I didn't understand her, it still sounded like wisdom.

Tommy loped up, hanging onto the horn. A real cowboy never hangs onto the horn. Old Buster was covered in sweat. Both of them looked happy to stop.

"Whew, you guys," Tommy panted.

Irma got down slowly and tightened up the saddle straps around the horses' bellies. She always did that after the first run because sometimes the horses let out gas and the straps loosened. If our saddle slipped on a gallop, we'd fall and get our heads kicked in. Then it would just get messy with Mother, and I'd never get to be a cowboy.

Irma started to climb back on Cesar, but she got face-twisted, like something hurt. She rubbed her knee.

"Irma?" I said.

"Time for a breather," she said.

Usually, our boots never touched the ground until we got back to the barn. But Irma unstrapped Tommy from his saddle and set him down. I swung my legs over the horn so I was sitting sidesaddle, edging down. I tried to ignore the dizzy feeling. Irma's grip around my waist gave me a soft landing.

She let us drink from her striped Indian blanket canteen. It smelled like old people's breath. Irma gimped over to the oak, sat down, and pressed her back against it. She straightened her legs slowly into an unladylike spread.

"This oughta ease up in a bit," she said.

She shoved a tobacco chaw in her mouth that bulged her cheek like a big bee sting.

"I have to be excused," said Tommy, and headed for a stand of trees.

"Don't squat with your spurs on," I shouted.

It wasn't often that I got try out my cowboy humor from Cousin Herb and the Trading Post Gang.

The cicadas were buzzing. The sun heated up. My Levi's felt hot to the touch.

Irma rested against the oak, hat over her face. I fed Ranger my last sugar cube and combed his mane with my fingers.

Tommy strolled out of the trees.

"Your barn door's open," I said.

He looked down and zipped his fly.

"Is Irma sick?" said Tommy.

"Just napping," I said.

He whispered, "She looks dead."

Irma sat up. The hat fell off her face and into her lap like she'd done a circus trick. For a moment she didn't seem to know us. Then she got herself standing in fits and starts.

Irma got us mounted up and then led Cesar next to a stump so she could climb on easier. It still looked painful the way her old face scrunched up. She took us the fast way home—a farm road past maize fields on one side and alfalfa on the other. Monarch butterflies floating all around us yellowed the air.

I noticed Irma wasn't sitting straight in the saddle like she'd taught us to do. More of an old-person slump. What if she was dying? I had to hurry up and fall off before it was too late. Irma was the only one who could tell if I was a real cowboy.

I held on to the saddle horn with my right hand and leaned way to the left, ready to let go and fall. When I looked down for a soft spot to land, the ground broke up into a million pieces. Vertigo again. I felt sick and sweaty. What would John Wayne do? I stared at the horizon of trees.

I still couldn't let go. Maybe if I socked myself in the jaw as hard as I could, then I'd fall.

Ranger looked back at me angling out from the saddle. He snorted, and I straightened up and wiped my eyes with my sleeve.

If I had a gun, I'd shoot myself for being such a chickenshit.

It was noon when we finally rode out of the narrow trailhead. The shadows had disappeared around Irma's trailer and the red barn had turned pale in the change of light.

Our horses knew where to stop inside the practice ring. They snorted and stomped for their oats. Irma slid off slow. She unbuckled Cesar's saddle and let it fall to the ground like she didn't have the strength to hold it up. Seemed like she could really use some help.

"Big Jim not here?" I said.

She shook her head.

Sometimes Big Jim helped us down. He was this huge guy who lived down the road with piles of shot-up bottles in his front yard. Irma said he used to wear a pistol in his belt until it blew his knee off. He gimped around on thin bowed legs like Irma's. But he was mean. Once he took me into the barn and made me roll cigarettes for him until I got it right.

"Irma," I said. "Big Jim's coming."

She stood up straighter and watched him.

Big Jim gimped out of the barn toward us, buttoning the top of his dirty Levi's. His leather belt, with a big metal rodeo buckle, hung open under his belly.

Big Jim passed Irma without looking at her and tripped toward me. The beery stink of him came straight up my nose.

"Hey, you, city slicker," Big Jim slurred.

"Their riding's done, Jim," Irma said to his back. "You got them oats ready?"

He stuck my dangling boot back in the stirrup. Tommy sat stiff as a corncob on Buster.

"She learn you to trot yet?" said Big Jim.

"Irma says trotting weakens the liver," I said.

"Well say good-bye to your liver, Miss Smarty-Pants," he said.

Big Jim pecked at my leg with his fingers.

"Jim, leave her be." Irma took a step toward him. "You go on home. And buckle up your belt."

Big Jim took off his filthy Stetson. I thought it was surrender. Then he swatted at Ranger's butt, and then Buster's.

"GIT! GIT, YOU PANSIES!" he shouted.

Both our horses lunged for the other side of the practice ring. Tommy yelled and held on.

Big Jim whipped off his belt, spinning the buckle over his head. He charged after us, rooster-eyed crazy.

"Trot, ya pansies!" yelled Big Jim

"Jim! Goddam it!" hollered Irma.

Irma limped after him, but she couldn't get close with Big Jim's belt whizzing in the air.

"TROT!" yelled Big Jim.

Ranger was already sidestepping as far from that belt as he could get. I nudged him into a trot and tried to stand high enough in the stirrups so the saddle wouldn't whack my tenders. I couldn't get in synch with Ranger's hard ups and downs. It was pure torture.

Jim's big belly followed us around the ring like a bulging eye. He swung the belt in wide loops over his head so we wouldn't stop.

I bounced like water bubbles on hot grease. I heard little brother bawling behind me. I looked back and shouted. "Stand up!"

Tommy's sneakers had lost their stirrup foothold. His little red mouth was open and wet. His head jolted up and down, neck snapping like he was in one car wreck after another. He held tight to the saddle horn. Then he vomited on himself. Mother was going to kill me!

Big Jim kept swinging his belt.

"Damnit, Jim!" Irma hollered. "You know what happens if I get the sheriff out here again!"

Big Jim raised a fist. "I'll break yer skull, Ma!"

Ma? Holy crap!

Irma gimped out of the ring and headed for the tack room phone. Big Jim followed her to the gate, screaming his head off.

I reined in Ranger. Old Buster stopped right behind me.

"Jump off!" I said to Tommy. "Quick!"

He unstrapped himself from the saddle and slid off. His pony was close to the ground, so he didn't land too hard.

"Come on, Sis!" said Tommy.

He scooted under the fence and out of the practice ring.

I was trying to wedge off, trying not to look down, but I got nightmare dizzy.

Big Jim stood blocking the open gate, his back to me, still hollering at Irma. If I could ride right by him, I could get to Irma. She'd help me down and I'd be safe.

I leaned forward, scared to death. "Let's go, boy!"

I kicked Ranger, heading for the other side of the practice ring.

Big Jim must've heard us coming. He whipped around. Eyes wild. When we got close, he swung hard. The belt buckle hit Ranger solid in the face. He reared up and whinnied so shrill it hurt my ears. His mane flew back, whipped my face. I grabbed for the saddle horn, too late. I fell backward. Ranger's hooves danced panic. My head hit the earth full force.

When I opened my eyes, Irma's fingers were checking out my bones. My head felt like it wasn't on straight anymore. It was hard to breathe.

Tommy's face was close.

"Easy, Sis," he said. "You might have a concussion. You fell off hard."

I hurt so bad I didn't know if I could even stand up. Little by little Irma helped me until I was on my feet. It felt like I'd broken just about everything.

Tommy's words floated back to me. "You fell off hard."

I had fallen! I had finally fallen off!

Irma always said that getting back on was the measure. I didn't hurt so bad that I couldn't get back on. All I had to do was mount up and I was a real cowboy!

"Where's Ranger?" I said.

Irma pointed with a nod of her head.

He was clear on the other side of the ring, as far away from us as he could get.

Blood dripped down his face. That whinny of pain, when the belt struck, still rung in my ears. He looked at me, like, *Why*? Why would anyone do that to him? Those big brown eyes broke my heart.

"Ranger, good old boy," I said, taking a step toward him.

His head went up, ears back. Eyes wide. A wild look.

"Stay put." Irma held me. "Beat-up horse, don't trust like they did. He'll need some vet stitching is all."

Irma's grip was strong, and the fight was out of me. I let her take me toward the gate, when all I wanted to do was throw my arms around Ranger's neck.

At the gate, Big Jim was flopped down flat on his back like a tired animal. Shirt open, blotched yellow belly to the sky.

Irma put her boot on Big Jim's wrist and took that rodeo belt out of his hand. He looked up at us and let out a big belch. Ranger gave a low whinny. I wanted to stomp Big Jim's head in.

A police siren wailed across the Kern River Bridge. Irma looked in the direction of the sound. She let out a long sigh and turned to us.

"You'd best not come again," she said, in a voice flat as a prairie.

Her words hit me like a fist.

"But Irma, I have to. You said that the measure of a cowboy was getting back on!"

"I taught you good enough, Rodeo," she said.

Rodeo? She called me Rodeo!

Irma's round roast body limped away. Everything that made me feel six feet tall was leaving with her.

I heard Mother's horn honk.

I looked over at Ranger bleeding, Big Jim passed out, Tommy stinking of vomit.

Mother honked again.

Tommy took my hand and tugged me toward the path. It felt good to hang onto something.

We walked slowly, but my heart was pounding. I felt Ranger's big, thundering body under me. Ranger and me, galloping past the cottonwood and giant willows, the wind in our faces and the sun on our backs, riding to save the town, headed for glory, faster and faster, and the bad guys never get us.

CHAPTER 6
RICKY THE PERV

God, I could use some adult conversation!
—Mother

Bakersfield, June 1953

I yawned and threw my knife on the kitchen table. "I'm sick of this!" I said.

All morning long, Tommy and I had been carving dumb designs in raw potatoes, dipping them in paint and stamping them on butcher paper. It looked like rows of squished bugs.

"We've done enough to wallpaper a gym," I said. "I'm bored!"

"You're not allowed to be bored," said Mother. "If this doesn't suit you, read a book. Or write one. It's only people without inner resources who give in to boredom."

She poured herself some lemonade. "God," she said, clutching the glass, "I could use some adult conversation."

Her inner resources weren't doing much better than mine, now that Daddy had hired a full-time secretary and Mother was full-time with us.

Mother had tried joining the League of Women Voters for stimulation. But that only lasted until she heard some of the ladies say, there was something wrong with her brain because she was a Democrat.

Mother used to have a highly competitive weekly bridge club in her old San Francisco days. Here, in Bakersfield all she could find was Bridget the romance magazine writer, who was a pretty distracted player and Harriet, a snob who had something gossipy to say about everyone. That was kind of fun. Elly, a short-haired helicopter pilot, was my personal favorite. She dressed and swore like a guy, and hogged the conversation with wild stories about running guns during the Suez conflict. She promised to take me up in her Bell 47 single-rotor someday.

Mother's only other Bakersfield distraction was Hart Park. She'd drive us out to the lake for a picnic to remind herself just how good it felt to leave Bakersfield. Tommy and I tossed our bread crusts to the ducks, and Mother would stare at the horizon with a far-off look in her eyes.

Today she had that same Hart Park stare.

After cleaning up the art mess, I went out in the backyard and sat in my tumbleweed fort where I liked to think. I tried to imagine what I could do to make Mother feel better.

I looked up past the tumbleweeds and noticed our neighbor, Ricky Weak, climbing into his fig tree. He eased into a pissed-off slouch with a comic book. Something about his freckled frowning face always made me want to be his friend. When we'd moved into the neighborhood, his family never howdied or casseroled us like other neighbors on the block. I watched him read for a while, and then I hollered.

"Hey! Wanna see my tumbleweed fort?"

He didn't even look up. "I don't play with little kids."

Little kids? I was ten! I bet he wasn't more than twelve.

I picked a couple of our snapdragon flowers and stuck them up my nose. Even with purple nostrils I couldn't get Ricky's attention. But it gave me an idea.

I ran inside. Mother was drying the dishes.

"You want adult conversation?" I said. "How about inviting the Weaks over for dinner?"

"I'm not *that* desperate," said Mother.

Then she looked out the window and sighed heavily. "Yes, I am."

After a while, she sat down and wrote an invitation on a piece of butcher paper. She left the note taped to their front door for Saturday night dinner at 6:00.

We got a note back on our front door the next day saying: "Glad to accept. There are four of us. Pauline."

Mother was more excited than I'd seen her in a while. Now she had something special to look forward to. Saturday came and we cleaned the house. That took us half the day. By five o'clock we'd set the table.

I dressed up in my new red shirt and clipped my hair back with a big shiny barrette.

Mother put store-bought roses in her best vase in the middle of our best tablecloth. The steak-and-potato dinner with sweet corn was done by five-thirty. We wrapped everything in foil to keep it warm. Mother liked to say she was an on-time person who'd rather have everything ready than tasty. She even bought a gallon of vanilla ice cream for the guests. Tommy and I were rarely allowed sweets because Mother didn't want dentists in our lives.

At 5:35 Daddy called and said he had to do an emergency operation at the hospital. A biker had left part of his skull on the highway. Daddy was always puzzling bikers back together.

At six we were waiting in the front room for the Weaks. Tommy and I played Go Fish on the couch. Mother paced a bit and opened the front door. It got to be half-past six.

"My nightmare scenario," she said. "Give a party and no one comes. I don't even have their phone number."

She turned and stared at the dining room table. She sighed.

"Oh well! Come on and help me," she said.

We started to pick up the plates. A loud knock at the backdoor nearly scared the bejesus out of us. In walked Mrs. Weak, alone. No Ricky. She was hugging a bottle of Jack Daniels. Her thick curly red hair was bunched high on her head. A silky blouse had slipped off her shoulder so you could see a bra strap. Her boobs were like baby pink pigs curled on her chest.

"Sorry, all," she said. "Hank got a call from his boss and took off on his rig. My mother has the runs, so you don't want her here. Loving son Ricky is not one for company. So here I am. And call me Pauline!"

Being late was rude. But in Mother's book, being *this* late was a crime. Still, she switched quick to her party face. I tried mine on too. We got busy serving up the lukewarm dinner. As we sat down to eat, Mother did something I knew she hated, asking questions when she didn't care about the answer. She called it "really small talk." It didn't take much to get Pauline going. She talked, ate, and drank enough to make up for everyone who wasn't there.

She told us there were three things we wanted to know about her: she was a graduate of Eve's Hair Salon, she did great cuts, and she was tit-deep into Raymond Chandler. With a big smile, she described the bloody murder story she was reading. Steak churned behind her teeth. And then she told us some sex stuff in the book. She called it *steamy*.

I guessed this was the adult conversation Mother wanted so bad. At least she didn't excuse us kids from the table. I wouldn't have left anyway. There were a lot of new words that I wanted to look up.

When we got to the ice cream, Pauline drizzled booze from her glass over her scoops and then poured some from the bottle on Mother's ice cream.

"I don't drink," said Mother.

Pauline didn't seem to care and made quite a puddle in their bowls. I scarfed down my rare ice cream treat and watched Mother taste her boozy vanilla mound. I think she surprised herself by liking it because she finished it off. They both had seconds. Pretty soon everything Pauline said made Mother laugh. Being silly and laughing was a whole new Mother. She seemed younger and more fun, the kind of person I'd like for a friend.

Next morning, Mother was slower than her real self. During breakfast we heard a loud knock at the backdoor. Mother touched her forehead. Pauline came in carrying her own cup of steaming coffee and a bouquet of white daisies.

"I don't mean to get above my raising," said Pauline, stuffing her flowers in my water glass, "but I'm inviting myself over to play cards."

The next morning, and the next, and the one after that, Mother and Pauline drank coffee and played gin rummy. I'll be darned if they didn't have a lot to say to each other. Or at least Mother didn't seem to mind listening to Pauline run off at the mouth. Mother said that she looked forward to their morning routine, even if Pauline's Camel cigarettes smoked up our kitchen.

Tommy and I left them alone because they were boring. We'd been meaning to dig to China anyway. We carried our shovels into the backyard. Ricky was slouched in his fig tree. Just to annoy him, I sent Tommy to ask him if he wanted to help us dig to China.

"Screw you, Chink lover!" Ricky snapped.

That made no sense.

"Hey!" I said. I strutted up to the hedge with my shovel. "No one talks to my brother like that!"

"You stink!" he yelled.

Wow, this guy was really bad at insult war. "Screw you," I said.

"Ma says you're Jews," he said. "Lemme see your horns."

Tommy and I looked at each other. Horns? Not a compliment.

"Well, your Mom's a big booby cow!" I hollered back.

His face went as red as his hair. Ricky pulled a knife out of his belt. Not a pocketknife like I had in my Levi's, but a real knife that could kill those skinny chickens that crapped up his yard.

"Maaaaaaa!" Tommy's fat legs scrammed toward the back door.

I stood steady with my shovel ready for a fight. Ricky slid out of the tree. His knife flashed like a sharp stab of sunlight.

I dropped my shovel and ran. He leapt the fence and came after me.

Mother burst out of the screen door with a metal pancake flipper. Ricky saw her, skidded to a halt, and ran home.

Mother was steaming. Pauline promised she would frisk her son for weapons before allowing him out of the house. They both agreed that Ricky and I should not play together. Thank you! What a freak!

Next day I took a walk down Butler Street looking for some fun. A few kids were playing jacks in their driveway. Boring. Down the block a bunch of other kids about my age were forming up for football. The best-looking blond man I ever saw was showing them how to tackle. I couldn't take my eyes off his muscles.

"Can I play too?" I said.

"You're a girl," said the blond man, grinning.

"Watch me!" I said. "I'll murder these guys."

They called him Coach. I was there every single day. He liked it when I called him Tarzan. He asked us to toughen up his son Burt, who was about my age, but a real wimp. So, I tackled the kid harder than anyone, because Coach said a tackle should hurt the other guy. I was good at it.

After one game everyone left crying but me. Coach patted my shoulder with his big hand. "Wish you were my son," he said.

Wait a minute. I didn't want to be his son. I wanted to marry him.

But Tarzan's wife called off coaching because Burt was getting grass stains on his clothes and bruises everywhere.

Without Coach, summer got boring all over again. I wandered down the street, sizing up tumbleweeds for my tumbleweed fort. But none of them looked big enough.

So, when Ricky hollered at me from his lawn and said, "Hey, wanna see a secret?"

I said, "Sure!"

I'd promised Mother never to play with Ricky again, but what kid says no to a secret?

Ricky started down Butler. I guess he expected me to follow. My thinking went like this: Mother would be making lunch, so that would take a little while. I wasn't digging to China today because Daddy had filled our hole. So, I followed Ricky. And followed. I didn't know the secret was so far away. I'd never been more than six blocks from the house without Mother.

Ricky led me to a fancy park I'd never seen before. No kids were playing on the swing sets or jungle gyms. No grown-ups were wandering around. Where was everyone? I followed Ricky along a path with new flower plantings, huge maples, clean wooden picnic tables, and little barbecue grills. Boy, I'd never seen a park this deserted.

In the middle of the park was a big outdoor theater. Without waiting for me, Ricky ran up the steps, crossed the stage and disappeared behind some Greek columns. I climbed up on the stage and twirled, just to get that center-of-attention feel.

"Ricky!" I yelled. No answer.

Was he the kind of creep who would leave me here for a bad joke?

"Where are you, asshole?" I shouted.

I got a little panicky. I didn't know how to get home. We'd passed a phone booth on the sidewalk. But I didn't have a dime to call Mother. What was our number? And where was I anyway?

I ran through the Greek columns where Ricky had gone. Backstage had a big nook with a statue of a robed guy holding a book. In the other nook, was Ricky standing naked. Facing me. His skinny body was covered in freckles.

I choked. I stared. I shouldn't have. His ding-dong was bigger than little brother's, but way smaller than a horse's. His clothes were piled in a heap next to him. Ricky tossed his leather belt at my feet. It had Indian beads sewn on.

"You have to play the game with me," he said.

"What game?"

He turned his back to me. A wobbly butt. But also, holy crap! Ugly red scars on his back. Who did that to him?

"It's just a game," he said. "Hit me with the belt. It's OK. Go ahead."

Was he kidding? Why would anyone *want* a whipping? His butt tightened. He was waiting. Why did he think I would do it? Did he see me tackle Burt?

"Pick it up," said Ricky in a scratchy voice.

"You're not a statue," I said. I was shaking now. What I meant to say was, "Put your clothes on and take me home!"

His freckled back shook. I heard his sobs.

"God wants you to!" He was crying. "Please! It makes me clean!"

My knees wobbled so bad I could barely stand. I threw the belt back at him. He picked it up. Was he going to come after me? Then he started whipping his own backside hard. I felt sick seeing those healed welts turn bloody.

Shaking all over, I turned and ran back through the columns, down the stairs, and bolted through the park. I was crying past all those picnic tables and didn't see the man on the path. I ran smack into him. He was fat and dressed in shorts and a Hawaiian shirt. He wasn't very good-looking.

"What's wrong with you?" he said. He stepped back.

Mother always said, "Never talk to strangers." I tried to snort back my tears.

"I'm lost," I said.

"Where do you live?" he said. I liked his voice. It was soft and low.

Where did I live? He was eating an orange and handed me a slice.

Mother always said, "Never take anything from strangers."

I choked on the juice. Then I remembered. Mother had sewn address labels for camp into our collars. I showed the man where the clue was. He bent close and turned my collar out. His fingers smelled like oranges.

Mother always said, "If a strange man touches you, run!"

His breath was warm on my neck. I shivered.

"Here it is," he said. "Not far. I'll take you home."

The man wiped his hands on his shorts.

Mother always said, "Never go anywhere with a strange man, or you'll end up dead in a dark alley."

I'd broken all Mother's rules and now I was going to die.

He grabbed my hand. His grip was strong. He walked us out of the park, across the busy street and past some fancy houses. None of them looked familiar. I didn't even know if we were headed in the right direction.

The tears started rolling down my cheeks. Mother would be so pissed when they found my strangled body. Then I saw the Gradys' green house. I knew that house! And their bulldog, Icarus! We'd just come from a different way. That meant we were only a couple blocks away from my house.

"I know where I live!" I yelled.

I jerked my hand out of his and raced like mad down the street. Mother was outside and grabbed me up in a big hug, the kind you don't get anywhere else.

"Where were you?" she said. "I've been looking for you!"

She peeled me off her neck as she stood up. The man had followed me. He came up and said his name was Stan. Even with his steady voice, it took some doing to calm Mother down. He told her that I was a real trooper and knew how to ask for help. He wasn't as bad-looking as I thought. Just fat in the stomach.

Mother thanked him over and over. When he'd gone, she took me into the kitchen for my milk and sandwich. She kept asking where I'd been.

"I went for a walk and got lost and ended up in the park," I said.

I guess she could tell there was more. All I really wanted was for her to stop asking me questions. I wanted to climb into her lap, sit safe, and never leave the house again.

The Weaks' creepy secret was going to have to be my creepy secret now. I couldn't tell Mother the truth. She needed a friend more than I did.

CHAPTER 7
GHOST WEDDING

Would you want someone biking on Grandpa's grave?
—Mother

Bakersfield, September 1953

After school, I pulled on my T-shirt and Levi's, jumped on my blue Schwinn, Romeo, and pumped quick as lightning to the Chinese graveyard.

It was a few acres, with a tall bluff and sunken graves. We kids kicked up dust clouds with our wheelies. Not that we were a real gang, but this was our territory. When we had something to prove, or an argument came up, we'd settle it by riding over the edge of the bluff, angle full tilt down the steep slope, picking up speed. It was a struggle to stay upright to the bottom in that soft graveyard dust.

Every once in a while, someone got something stuck in their spokes and landed hard. But not as hard as the kid who got his arm broken. The parents tried to stop us.

Mother warned me. "If you get hurt, say good-bye to Romeo. It's not just dangerous, it's disrespectful. Would you want someone biking on Grandpa's grave?"

Far as we knew, no Chinaman had been buried there for over a hundred years, not since they finished building the railroad. It was as abandoned as a haunted house. We had the whole place to ourselves with no grown-ups nosing around. Besides, if the dead cared about us hooting around, wouldn't they have spooked us off by now?

It was a steep pump on the trail from the sidewalk up to the bluff. I was panting by the time I reached the gang. They were leaning on their bikes in a loose circle jabbering under the big oak. I rode closer and bumped Candy's tire. You could tire-bump a pal and not start something.

"What's what?" I said.

She didn't bump back, not this time. Candy's green eyes were focused on this Chinese guy biking toward us on a Schwinn Whizzer. There were about ten cards clipped to his spokes making a big racket.

Everything about him was so cool. He was older, maybe high school. His black wig chop was a spiffy DA. And the way the cig drooped from his lips, and a beat-up bomber jacket that was too big for him. It could've belonged to his dad. Lots of kids had dead dads from the war.

It was gutsy, him coming up here alone. I'd never seen anyone in the graveyard who wasn't white. Kids pretty much divided up by color in the neighborhood, just like on the playground. At recess Chinese kids hogged the tetherball and beat everyone. Mexican kids hung out at the jungle gym. No colored kids went to our school, but we had the Basques. Their parents owned noisy restaurants where everyone had to sit at one long table to eat. There weren't many Jews. But we got called names too. Nothing razzed my berries worse than kids shouting "kike." I shouted their ugly punk names back at them. You really had to stand up for yourself on the playground or you were dead meat.

The Chinese guy was looking us over like we were insects.

"This is a Chinese cemetery," he said. "You're trespassing. All of you, get out of here now!"

We just stood and stared back at him. Who the hell did this guy think he was dealing with? We weren't going anywhere.

"This is our turf," said Wayne Bob. He was the biggest kid in our class and famous for his knuckle sandwich. "We been coming up here for a year, so that dibs it."

We crowded closer, backing up Wayne Bob.

The Chinese guy reached for his back pocket, like he was going to pull a knife. But instead, he whipped out a big plastic comb. He slicked back his dark hair and raised the comb above his head. He whacked the teeth hard on the top of his other hand. It made dents. Deep dents. It was the old comb trick, but he did it harder. Then he spun his arm like he was winding up for a pitch, and just kept going and going in a circle, until blood oozed out of the dents on the top of his hand.

He held up his bloody fist.

"This is your face, bozo," he said. "You take your shitty little friends out of here now!"

Candy and I looked at each other. Holy cow! No one ever stuck it that hard to Wayne Bob. But Wayne Bob stuck it right back.

"Look, prick," said Wayne Bob, "you want us out? You and me ride over that bluff. When you land on your ass, you're the one that's outta here."

The Chinese guy inhaled a long drag on his cigarette and blew the smoke out slowly.

"When I don't land on my ass," he said, "all you get out and never come back."

"Deal!" Wayne Bob gripped his handlebars like fury. "We'll show him, right guys?"

"Yah!" we said. That was settled. Wayne Bob was the best.

Wayne Bob rode to edge of the bluff. We gathered around to watch like we had a million times. He edged his front wheel over the crumbly rim, took a breath, and shot off down the steep slope. His wheels spun fast. Spokes churned the loose dirt. Wayne Bob made it to the bottom and skidded to a halt sideways before his tires hit the concrete sidewalk. Not one of his best rides, but we cheered him.

We turned to make room for the Chinese guy to hike his bike up to the edge. But he sneered and flicked the smoking butt at my tire. He walked his Whizzer way far back from the rim, jumped on and pumped hard toward us.

Those ten cards clipped to his spokes sounded like a DC-7 taking off. We stepped back to give him room. His wheels shot off the edge.

I held my breath to help him. His speed took him out into the air. He whooped, hands thrown up for a second. Then, he landed halfway down the slope in a big explosion of dust. His legs pumped and he skidded to a fancy stop, tires spraying dust all over Wayne Bob.

Jesus! That had to be the best ride in our history. I wanted to clap for him. But no one did. The guy stood straight-legged and looked up at us. Beautiful white teeth in a smile that wasn't a smile. He shouted so we all heard.

"My name's Louie. I'm going to get my gang. If you're still here when we get back, we'll cut your eyeballs out."

Jesus. That was scary. We watched him ride off down the street. Wayne Bob threw a dirt clod. It didn't land anywhere near Louie. Nobody said anything. I bet we were all thinking the same thing. Wayne Bob had let us down. He was the first to ride off, head down, shoulders around his thick ears.

There was no one left to fight for us, so we had to leave. It was almost like someone had died, that's how bad it felt. Crap! The Chinese graveyard was the best part of my day. It was just us kids screwing around, free as could be.

As the sky got darker, we said our sad good-byes to each other. Before I could leave, Candy tire bumped me.

"Hey, what's up?" I said.

"That guy, Louie," said Candy. "He threw his cigarette at you."

I knew where this was going. She'd suddenly gotten boy-crazy, and it was making me nuts. What was the big deal? Boys were just people like us, only not as smart.

"Christ, you can have him," I said.

"I dare you to wait for him," said Candy.

"Right, and his gang," I said. "Who needs eyeballs?"

She snickered. "No really, wait for him." She made a kissy sound and pumped off on her bike fast, like I was going to chase her.

To hell with that. I loved being up here by myself. Almost any place was improved without people in it.

There was barely enough light to keep ghosts shy, so I rode along the dusty trail for home and felt the night close in on my back. A faded moon balloon floated above the eucalyptus trees. Fog rose from the damp graves. I turned one last time and saw something move at the big oak. Crap! Before I could speed up, Louie came at me.

How'd he get back here so fast? He skidded to a stop and leapt off his bike in front of me.

"What the hell are you still doing here!" he yelled.

He was big enough to block the moon.

"I'm going! I'm going!" I said.

But right behind his shoulder, in the distance, there was a weird light coming our way.

I almost choked on my spit. "Your gang!"

He turned to look. "Oh, shit!" he said. "Now, it's too late."

Louie looked as scared as I was. He grabbed my arm and dragged me off Romeo down into a caved-in grave. There was broken crap under our knees that smelled old and musty. I tried to pull away, but he held on to my arm.

Louie looked above the rim of the sunken grave. I sat up and looked too. In a long stretch of rising fog was a small orange glow. Another glow followed the first. Finally, another one, dim enough to be my imagination.

"Ghosts?" I whispered.

Louie was breathing like he'd run a race.

The soft lights floated closer and closer toward the black leafless oak.

"What are those lights?" I said.

"I swear, I'll slit your throat if you don't shut up," he hissed.

The strange glowing multiplied, from two to three, then four, moving closer. Shadows plowed through the rising fog. A sweet tinging of bells echoed in the darkness. Figures floated legless only yards from the oak and from us. Robes turned into human forms.

I was trembling. "Louie, who are they?" I whispered.

"Shut up," he whispered. "The family can't know you're here."

Family?

Their silky costumes reflected in the dim lantern light. The tall one turned his lantern brighter, and I saw all their faces.

Jesus Christ! It was Mr. and Mrs. Wong from the China Bowl Restaurant where we ate on Sundays and Christmas. I loved their food! And Mr. and Mrs. Ping from Ping's Laundry. Mrs. Ping taught me how to say *no starch* in Mandarin. I knew their everyday smiles. But now they looked unreal, like a play.

"I know your family," I whispered. "They know my family. Why are we hiding?"

"You're *gweilo*." He looked like he wanted to kill me.

Mr. Ping banged a small drum that sounded like a soft heartbeat. Mrs. Wong rubbed a bow across a stringed instrument. The music was squeaky. All four moved together, each taking a part. Like a dance, but not a dance.

Mr. Wong and Mr. Ping unfolded a life-sized paper man and stuck him upright with slim bamboo poles. Lantern light glowed through the colorful rice-paper man, making him look like a stained-glass window.

A young, beautiful Chinese woman stepped out of the darkness. She was wearing a shining golden headdress and shimmering robe. She stood still as a statue next to the paper man. Mr. Wong sprinkled them with gold confetti.

Everyone bowed their heads for a minute. Mr. Ping said something in Chinese and it looked like they were praying. Then he lit the paper man on fire. It flamed bright with the different colors reflecting on their robes. The paper man turned to ash and embered upward into a draft of oak branches and moonlight.

The young woman put her hand to her mouth and her body shook. Maybe she was crying. Then it seemed the ceremony was over because the Wongs and Pings and the young woman turned down the lanterns' light and walked back the way they'd come, slowly becoming shadows again.

I let my breath out and rubbed my arm where Louie had gripped me so tightly.

By now, Mother might have the cops out. I climbed quickly out of the grave and grabbed Romeo. Louie picked up his Whizzer.

"If you tell anyone what you saw," he said, "I'll hunt you down and kill you."

He'd be so good-looking if he wasn't always frowning.

"Who'd believe me?" I said. "Louie, wait. I mean, Jesus Christ, what was that?"

He took a deep breath and spoke quickly. "It's called a *Minghun*. A ghost wedding. If the groom dies before the ceremony, the bank accounts of the two families can still get married. It's legal. The ceremony has to take place out here, among the ancestors so as not to offend them. I was assigned to get rid of you creeps so you wouldn't dishonor my family by seeing what is not yours to see. You *gweilos*, you have no shame!"

"What the hell is a *gweilo*? Does that mean you hate me because I'm Jewish?"

"Jewish?" He brushed off his leather jacket. "No, I hate you because you're white."

I was so used to being hated for being a Jew, that being hated for being white was kind of refreshing.

Louie hopped on his bike and took off fast in the direction that the Wongs and Pings had gone. I pedaled fast across the graveyard, headed for home.

I felt bad that Romeo's tires were riding over Louie's family's bones. I thought about Grandpa's bones in the Jewish cemetery. What if all the Chinese bones and Jewish bones got together. I bet everyone would look the same. Bone for bone, no one would know who to hate at recess.

I pedaled faster. Hell was waiting for me at home.

CHAPTER 8
THE VISITATION

Just follow my list.
—Mother

Bakersfield, July 1954

Mother paced back and forth in the kitchen over her spotless linoleum.

"Daddy should be back by now," she said.

She grabbed another cup of black coffee, as if that would calm her down.

She looked at the kitchen clock, her wristwatch, then paced again in her nervous high heels.

"I told your grandmother to take an earlier bus," she said.

"It's not like they can get lost between here and the Greyhound station," I said.

But nothing I said ever helped once Mother's panic button was pushed.

I looked out the kitchen window. The street was empty. The sky was a late-afternoon red.

There were only a few hours left before Mother and Daddy had to board the plane to Cuba. They needed to eat and the only restaurant at the Bakersfield Airport was called Terminal Dining. Besides, Grandma was bringing the beef.

I didn't blame Mother for being anxious. This was their big deal honeymoon. The one you're supposed to have when you get married. But back then, poor people like them just borrowed a car, drove to Yuma, Arizona, got married, and drove all the way back to Los Angeles. Who had money for a motel? Mother didn't even tell Grandma that she'd gotten married so that the family's annual Yosemite campout wouldn't be interrupted. While she was off hiking on Half Dome, Daddy found them an apartment so they could have kids.

For their late-in-the game honeymoon, they decided to splurge, now that Daddy was making a better living and we had this new home in the suburbs.

Mother wanted to boogie in Paris, but Daddy found a discount tour to the pleasure dome of Batista's Cuba. He loved to mambo.

I heard an engine and saw Daddy's Cadillac speeding up Spruce Street.

"Here they are" I said.

"Finally!" said Mother. "Can we please get this show on the road!"

Daddy cruised into the driveway. I rushed out the back door into a blast of late-afternoon heat.

Daddy gentled Grandma up out of the front seat. When she was solid on her short heels, I threw myself into her arms for a hug and buried my nose in the baby powder scent of her soft gray gabardine shoulder. When I came up for air, her smile was the sun. She held my face and kissed my cheek.

"*Sheyn kind*. Beautiful child," said Grandma, in her soft Yiddish accent.

Daddy grabbed her suitcase from the trunk. The three of us edged through the back door into Mother's kitchen, where she waited, arms folded.

"You're late, Mother," said Mother. Her voice made shame where there wasn't any.

"What can I say, darling?" Grandma said. "It's a bus."

Grandma never blamed anything for anything.

She set her big purse down on the polished linoleum and looked around.

"You got a beautiful new house," said Grandma. "Very nice. Much better than the other one."

Daddy looked pleased at the compliment. This Spruce Street ranch-style was a big step up from where we were on Butler Road.

Daddy excused himself and carried Grandma's suitcase to the back room.

Tommy ran in for a hug and showed Grandma his new book, *Lord of the Flies*. He said it made him want to be a writer or British.

Mother finally gave Grandma a hug, but they came apart faster than they'd come together, like bumper cars. Their eyes rested on me, the buffer.

Mother waved three stapled sheets of paper at Grandma.

"Everything you need to know is here, Mother," said Mother. "Just follow my list."

She put the list on the counter and yelled, "LENA!"

Lena scuffed into the room. Her dark bun was pulled so tight her cheekbones were shiny as apples. Her faded paisley dress was starched stiff. She'd taken off her apron. That's how we knew she'd dressed up.

"Yes, ma'am?" she said.

"Lena's been with us for a little while," said Mother. "She's Swedish, so she's very efficient at running the house."

Boy, wasn't that the truth. Every day, Mother would hand Lena a new list. Lena's loyalty to Mother's list was like her loyalty to Jesus. Keeping us "Christian clean," was how Lena put it.

"Lena," said Mother. "This is my mother, Mrs. Bertha Bannett."

"Miss Lena," said Grandma, holding out her hand. "Such a pleasure to meet you."

Grandma's hand, as she often reminded us, had shaken the hand of the great David Ben-Gurion, the first prime minister of Israel. He thanked her a lot in form letters because Grandma was a big *macher*

Zionist and a super fundraiser. Her speeches brought in money for Jews to buy land in Israel.

"After 4,000 years of getting the boot, Jews finally got a homeland!" said Grandma.

When she met Ben-Gurion in New York, he gave her a wooden gavel made from a dead Israeli olive tree.

"You can call me Grandma too, Miss Lena," said Grandma. "Everyone does."

Lena's face told us she would not be calling anyone Grandma.

"We have some last-minute details, Mother," said Mother, and headed for the bedroom to help Daddy get organized.

Grandma gave a happy little sigh of relief. She lifted her purse to the counter and pulled out a brisket wrapped in layers of heavy paper and plastic.

"From my butcher," she said. "Please, Miss Lena, may I have an apron?"

Lena was not happy letting Grandma take over the kitchen.

When Tommy and I set the table, Grandma said, "Set a place for Lena too."

That's not how we did things, but we didn't argue.

Grandma's reheated brisket filled our kitchen with the same terrific smell as her kitchen in Los Angeles. I'd spent a lot of time there with crayons. She'd made an art museum of my drawings scotch-taped to her white cupboards. It was easy to be a famous artist in Grandma's kitchen. Her house was a little bit magic because she hardly used electricity. Her refrigerator was just a metal box with a block of ice that got delivered twice a week. A black stove took wood and made real flames, not red coils. We listened to Caruso on her wind-up phonograph. When it ran slow, Caruso sounded like he was drowning.

On those warm Los Angeles afternoons at Grandma's house, instead of a regular nap, I got to rest on the thick blue carpet under her glass coffee table with a candy bowl on top. Grandma sat on the salmon-pink couch with white doilies on the armrests. A big window light behind her made a white halo of her hair. I shut my eyes so I could see the story she told. A plot made up just for me.

"Once upon a time," said Grandma, "a lovely Jewish giant named

Rachael was on her way through the forest. Wouldn't you know, she ran into Shlomo the hummingbird, who had a sore throat. Shlomo couldn't find a doctor anywhere. The poor bird was supposed to sing at the wedding of the princess. So, Rachael and Shlomo . . ."

Usually, I fell asleep and missed the ending, but she'd catch me up at bedtime in a Murphy bed the size of a swimming pool. I swam in the huge sheets. Behind the Murphy bed was a dark closet where Grandma stored American flags and boxes of her Jewish business papers. To help me sleep, she sat on the edge of the bed, stroking my forehead, singing with a voice that couldn't carry a tune. It was a Yiddish lullaby that her grandma had sung to her.

"Schlaf mein kind, schlaf mein kind." Sleep my child.

For some reason, Tommy was terrified of lullabies. But I fell very happily asleep, my hand resting on Grandma's knee.

Mother walked into the kitchen with her red lipstick around a smile.

"The brisket smells good, Mother," said Mother. "What's this?"

She picked up the extra plate I'd set on the table.

"So Lena should join us for the going-away dinner," said Grandma.

Lena stood in the doorway. "I never eat with the family."

Grandma smiled. "Miss Lena, you *are* family."

Lena turned and retreated to her room without a word. Mother put the extra plate back in the cupboard. That was the end of that.

Grandma's fall-apart-brisket and mashed potatoes were the big dinner hit. But her overcooked veggies, you could choke. Mother forked a wrinkled bean.

"Mother," said Mother. "How many times do I have to explain al dente?"

Boiling things to death was another Jewish legacy. When there wasn't any food in Daddy's Russian ghetto, he said his family boiled leather to chew. I bit my sandal once just to try it. You could break a tooth.

"Speaking of vegetables, darlings," said Grandma. She launched into one of her kibbutznik stories that always kept things pleasant.

"Did you know that the kibbutzniks in Israel grow giant vegetables? It takes two of them to pull up a turnip. Their olives are so big they're used for tractor tires. And children sleep in beds made from giant banana peels."

As the story got sillier, Grandma laughed more than the rest of us put together. Her laughter came from so deep that she had to hold on to the table so she wouldn't fall off her chair.

Two whole weeks with Grandma. I couldn't wait for the parents to leave.

After dinner Daddy loaded their Samsonite into the Yellow Cab. He gave me a big hug. Then he shook Tommy's hand.

"You're the man of the house now," he said.

Tommy stood up straighter, but he looked scared to death.

Mother's parting word to me was: "Behave."

Mother and Daddy climbed into the Yellow Cab and disappeared down the street.

Suddenly I felt like crying. What was wrong with me? I was afraid. What if they never came back from the pleasure dome of Batista's Cuba? What if they were secretly sick of me and decided to stay and dance the mambo forever? I felt Grandma's hand on my shoulder and the sadness slowly let go of my throat.

In the backroom, Grandma and I made up the pull-out bed. I sat in my pajamas watching her waltz to the radio music of Lawrence Welk while she hung up her clothes according to color, gray to black. Her flowered flannel nightgown floated around her like a circus tent. Finally, she sat on the bed with a jar of Ponds cold cream and rubbed it on her swollen red toes.

"This is my vegetable garden," she said with a laugh. "Onions, bunions, carrots, and tomatoes."

Grandma made everything better with a joke. She always said that there was no tragedy in things if you could laugh. "I think I clowned my life away," she said.

I wondered if she could help me with my Nazi nightmares. When they came, I was up all night, afraid to go back to sleep. Sometimes I thought I could hear tanks rolling down the street.

"Grandma," I said. "Do you think the Nazis will come again?"

"Sweetheart," she said. "Never waste time worrying before the catastrophe."

"But Grandma." I was almost in tears. "I dream the catastrophe almost every night."

She stroked my cheek with her cold cream hand.

"Bring me Zvi," she said.

Zvi was her big leather purse. A dead friend made it for her. Grandma took out her reading glasses, a notebook, and a fountain pen. I saw Mother's list crumpled in there too.

She put on her glasses. "Now," she said, "tell me your catastrophe."

She wrote it down and read it back to me:

"Hitler puts me in a gas chamber. The gas makes an awful hiss like a snake. I beat on the door to escape. I'm choking to death. Then I wake up sweaty, and my throat hurts."

She took off her glasses.

"Darling, when you change your words, you change your catastrophe." She handed me the pen and notebook. "Here. You're going write a *boem*."

Grandma wrote *boems*—bad poems—for the family birthdays.

Granddaughter, you're finally eleven.
I have a yen, a poem to send . . .

I settled her notebook in my lap. "But I'm not a good boet like you."

"Write," said Grandma. "Change the words. Something fun."

I held the pen tight and thought, and then I wrote.

In a gas chamber there is no kissing.
Only hissing.
Gas escapes like pissing.
A big wet blast.
From Hitler's ass.
He runs fast.

From his own gas.
And dies at last!

That felt good! Grandma was right.

"My granddaughter," Grandma said, laughing. "Such an imagination."

She hugged me.

"Dream sweet now, darling child," she said. "And always take care of your teeth."

She dropped her dentures into the water glass on the nightstand. They floated to the bottom in the glow of my Hopalong Cassidy nightlight.

We pulled the soft blanket over us. Through the curtains, a crack of Bakersfield moonlight made her wrinkled face look too old to be alive. I stared at Grandma's parted lips. I watched her breathing. A great responsibility. I wouldn't let Grandma die like Grandpa. There used to be two smiles in two glasses of water on the nightstand at her house. Grandpa called their teeth *The Cheshires afloat.* I called him Hot Lint, the smell he brought home from his tailor shop.

Grandma's snores filled the guest room. I snuggled close and breathed with her, in and out, until our breaths fell asleep together.

Another Bakersfield sunrise pressed against the curtain. I woke, my nose close to Grandma's face on the pillow. Her long white hair looked like angel wings. When she yawned awake for one more sunrise, it was such a relief.

The house was so much quieter now without Mother and Daddy. The kind of quiet when something is missing.

At breakfast, I inhaled the steam of white rice, hot milk, butter, cinnamon, and sugar. Tommy was grinning into his bowl as he ate. Butter slicked his chin. What Grandma did to rice, you could die from pleasure.

At the sink, Lena was polishing the silver hard enough to rub the shine off. She looked pissed.

Grandma noticed too. "Miss Lena, join us. Try my rice. It's an old family recipe I made up myself."

Lena wiped her hands, came over to the table, and stood above us frowning.

"My grandchildren in Arkansas thank Jesus for every bit of food," said Lena, "and sometimes they're still hungry. Your grandchildren eat their fill and never say one prayer of thanks to the Lord."

Those were more words than Lena had said in a month.

"This one." Lena nodded at me. "She took Jesus as her personal savior."

Grandma turned to me and raised an eyebrow. "You got a savior?"

I shrugged. Lena was such a tattletale.

"Miss Lena is right," said Grandma. "Children, each meal we're going to give thanks. Until your mother comes home. Sit up straight, sweethearts, not like *gruber yungs*."

Tommy and I sat up straight to show Grandma we weren't thugs.

"Come sit. Bring your rice, Miss Lena, and we'll pray with you."

Still frowning, Lena filled a bowl and sat down with us. She folded her hands and bowed her head. Grandma and Tommy bowed their heads. Mother always said we had to respect Lena's idiotic beliefs, so I bowed my head too.

"We thank you, God, for all the food we have been given at this table," said Grandma. "Thank you for my grandchildren's health, and the company of this nice Swedish woman, Miss Lena. May we all live to break bread in Israel."

"The Holy Land," Lena said softly.

"Yes," said Grandma, smiling at Lena. "The Holy Land."

The two old women looked at each other and said, "Amen," at the same time.

When we finished eating, Tommy and I leapt up, ready to go play.

Grandma pulled the small wooden gavel from Ben-Gurion out of her pocket and banged it lightly on the kitchen table.

"Now, my darlings, please sit," she said. "Welcome to the first meeting of the Bakersfield Kibbutzniks Board of Directors. We will vote on what we are going to do with our first day together. Ideas, please?"

"I'm finishing cleaning the silver," said Lena.

She returned to the sink with our empty bowls.

"I'm finishing *Lord of the Flies*," said Tommy, holding up his book.

"How about a game of gin rummy?" I said. "Or we can paint something together."

"Now, think," said Grandma. "What have you always dreamt of doing, if you had one special wish?"

I closed my eyes so I could see clearly. I'd always dreamt about running away from home, riding the rails, living in hobo jungles where there were no rules, ending up in Los Angeles, and becoming a famous movie star or artist or a cowboy. I'd live with Grandma in her big, yellow two-story on Normal Avenue in Los Angeles, where we had to be quiet because of the renter upstairs.

One time Jerry Lewis was shooting a scene on the campus across the street from Grandma's house. He let me sit in his chair with his name on the back. Someday when I got a chair with my name on the back, I'd return to Bakersfield. Then Mother would see that I could do a thing or two on my own.

"My dream is to run away from home," I said.

Grandma nodded.

But Lena looked confused. "Run away from what?" she said.

"Exactly!" said Tommy.

"Miss Lena," said Grandma. "What is your big dream before you die?"

Lena rinsed a pan and turned to Grandma.

Lena spoke slowly as though Grandma had a language problem. "I am busy with responsibilities."

"Come, come," Grandma said sweetly. "Give us your dream."

We sat in silence, waiting. Lena sighed.

"Before I die," she said, "I want to be received in the Holy Land."

"Great!" I said. "Let's run away to the Holy Land!"

Lena shook her head. "I don't understand how you people think."

"Look, it's easy," I said. "We hop a train, get off at the sea, and take a boat to the Holy Land. We'll be back before Mother gets home."

"Israel is not on your mother's list," said Lena. "Today is my special day. After I finish cleaning the silver, I'm going to spend it with my Lord."

"Hey," said Tommy. "What about my dream? To go nowhere."

Grandma got up from the table. "Children, come with me."

There was a secret in her voice.

We followed her into the backroom. She shut the door with a quiet click.

"It's Lena's birthday," she said. "And we're going to make her wish come true, to go to the Holy Land. First, we need an airline ticket. Go get your crayons."

I found Mother and Daddy's Pan Am receipts in their bedroom. I made a pretty good ticket as far as crayons get you. Passenger. Date. Destination. Round trip. Bakersfield to The Holy Land. Tommy looked over my shoulder.

"They'll never let her on the airplane," he said.

"Sweetheart, this is just pretend," said Grandma. "She'll never see Israel on her salary. We're going to take Lena someplace that we'll call the Holy Land."

"So, what's holy here, the Mojave Desert?" I said.

"Has Bakersfield got a delicatessen?" said Grandma.

"Luigi's Delicatessen is about six blocks away," I said.

"I'll treat her to lunch at the Holy Land of Luigi's," said Grandma. "We need presents."

"I could cut a cross out of colored paper," said Tommy.

"Perfect," said Grandma. "And you sweetheart, write her a boem."

"How do I write something for someone I hardly even like?" I said.

"Be brief," said Grandma.

An hour later, we found Lena sitting on her bed with her Bible open in her lap.

"Miss Lena," said Grandma. "We have a surprise for you on your special day."

I handed her the envelope.

Lena stared at us and then slowly opened the flap like there was a snake inside. She pulled out the fake ticket to The Holy Land, the cutout cross and the card from Grandma that said she was entitled to lunch at Luigi's.

"How did you know it was my birthday?" said Lena.

"Jews know these things," said Grandma.

I waved a sheet of paper.

"I wrote a boem for you," I said and cleared my throat. "For Lena and the Holy Land."

I hope you won't feel low.
We can only pretend to go.
Jesus knows you have no dough.
You are the best Christian I know.

Lena stared at me and at her gifts. She looked really uncomfortable.

"I'm confused," she said. "But thank you."

"Miss Lena," said Grandma. "The children and I would like to take you to a Holy Land lunch at Luigi's."

"Don't call Luigi's the Holy Land," said Lena. "That's a sacrilege."

She bowed her head, hands folded, maybe asking her Jesus for permission. Poor Lena. To live without an imagination. It was like being born without legs.

Lena stood up and took off her apron.

"I'm ready," said Lena. "When are we going?"

I was so shocked that she agreed, I almost fell over.

"Noon," said Grandma.

We scattered and grabbed what we needed for the six-block trek.

Everything I needed was in my Bermuda shorts. Gum, a pocketknife, a couple of purie marbles in case I ran into a game. Tommy put his book and a handful of Froot Loops neatly in a brown paper bag. We were walking there, so I told Grandma to wear one of Mother's light summer dresses because by noon it was 100 degrees outside.

"When your grandma goes out," said Grandma, "she doesn't shlep in a *schmatta*."

Looking good was such a family thing. You'd think they were raised rich. But Grandma and her two sisters, Rose and Ida, were raised in a Russian ghetto, and never got beyond a high school education. But somehow they knew operas by heart, quoted classic poems, and always dressed to the nines.

Every year, when the family gathered at Passover in Los Angeles, all of us cousins at the children's table got to watch our extroverted elders at their best; Grandma was the oldest sister and welcomed the family with a speech that had everyone laughing. Her religious sister, Rose, led the Passover ceremony that always went on way too long. But at least, we were all ready to eat by the time Ida, the pretty sister, oversaw the serving of the meal.

~

After two blocks in the blazing Bakersfield sun, Grandma's face was radish red. She clung to my shoulder and her matching purse. Her small heels dragged along the scorching pavement. Under the knit suit, she wore silk nylons and a rayon slip. Her one concession to the heat was to unbuttoned her jacket.

I walked slower and slower, in step with Grandma. Tommy waddled ahead, popping Froot Loops in his mouth. Lena seemed fine in her light cotton dress.

Finally, we pushed into the air-conditioned delicatessen. Luigi's was a good choice for the Holy Land. Grandma ordered us antipasto, bruschetta, Luigi's special ravioli, a salad, and red wine for the two ladies. Dessert was cheesecake, which Grandma said she did better. And a scoop of Geno's pistachio gelato with bits of chocolate.

This was first time I'd seen Lena eat from a plate instead a jar of our leftovers with ketchup like she did at home. Her dark eyebrows lifted with every bite.

Strangest of all, after a glass of Chianti, Lena and Grandma were talking like normal friends. How was that even possible? And stories I never knew. I was practically sitting in Grandma's lap so as not to miss one shred of the past.

Grandma said her first husband, Abraham Kaplan of Memphis, Tennessee, died in an auto accident. They'd only been married six months and she was pregnant with Mother, when *bang*. In one horrible moment, she had become a widow and a single mom, and worked in a dry goods store to support them. Eight years later, Mayer the tailor, the grandpa I knew, married Grandma and moved them from the South to a house on Normal Avenue in Los Angeles. I remembered him dancing the *kazatski* like a Cossack. Squatting, hands on hips, his legs shooting out in front of him. Grandma said Mayer was not as funny as Abraham. But he was a man with a big heart. He also had an older daughter of his own, who was unkind to Mother.

Mother had an ugly stepsister! Tell me more! Tell me more!

But Grandma wanted Lena to tell *her* story.

Getting Lena to talk about her family was like trying to squeeze glue from a dried-up tube. But, after some coaxing, and a second glass of Chianti, Lena's smile stretched a lot further than I knew possible in that boney face. She told us about the ones in her family who might make something of themselves, and finally, unbelievably, she laughed at one of Grandma's jokes. The sound burst out of her sudden and deep, like it had been stored for too long. A miracle in the Holy Land of Luigi's! If Grandma could convert Lena to laughter, she could change anyone's catastrophe. Maybe more people should have lunch with Grandma.

CHAPTER 9
RED HALLOWEEN

Dumb Dad. Dumb kid.
—Mother

Bakersfield, October 1954

Round as a donut and a few bricks shy of a load, nothing could hurry Arnie.

"We're leaving, lardo!" said Mary Ellen. "The other kids'll get all the good stuff!"

We'd been waiting way too long for her younger brother to get costumed up for Halloween.

Mary Ellen twirled toward the bedroom door and I followed. She was so graceful in her Tinker Bell tutu. Rouge covered her pale freckles and the glitter in her dark hair was like sparkly dandruff. This new Spruce Street neighborhood was full of cool kids, but she was the one I wanted for my best friend. She might be a hundred times prettier than me. But I was in my green Peter Pan costume, so we looked great together.

We're halfway out the bedroom door when Arnie yells. "No, wait! Watch this!"

He always yelled, "No wait. Watch this!" Then he'd do something anybody could do.

He unsnapped the pearl buttons of his cowboy shirt. His nipples were pink and smooth like Necco Wafers. His belly drooped over his Levi's.

"Ewwwww!" We chorused.

"No, wait! Come on. Watch this!" said Arnie.

He looped a thin leather strap around his fat neck. The strap was stapled to a small square of plywood. The square hung in the middle of his chest. He snapped his pearl button shirt over it.

"Ta-dum!" he said.

"So, what the hell, Arnie?" said Mary Ellen. "You're wearing a plywood necklace?"

"No! This is the best part, you guys!" said Arnie.

He scrabbled around on his cluttered desk and lifted a bone-handled hunting knife.

"That's Dad's!" said Mary Ellen.

"He won't mind," said Arnie.

"He sure too will mind!" said Mary Ellen.

Arnie put on his cowboy hat and raised the big hunting knife with two hands.

"I'm a cowboy zombie." He took a practice stab, barely touching the wood square on his chest with the tip of the knife. The move sucked our breath away.

"Arnie," I said. "Wouldn't it make more sense to stick the knife in the wood *before* it's on your chest?"

"I know what I'm doing, dick-breath," he said.

Mary Ellen nudged me. "Let him do it. It's the only way he learns."

He took that two-fisted grip and grinned at us. "Here goes for real!" he said.

As Arnie raised the knife, the wood square shifted. He sunk the knife into his chest. His eyes went wide. His mouth went *uh-oh*.

Arnie sat down hard on his guitar stool. Blood seeped into his pure white cowboy shirt.

When he tried to pull the knife out of his chest, he slid off the stool and fell on his back. His eyes fluttered like a couple of pinned butterflies.

We just stood there looking down at him. We were used to Arnie doing stupid things. Blood soaked into the braided rug under him.

He blinked up at us. "Daddy?" he gurgled.

I elbowed Mary Ellen. "Shouldn't we get your father?" I said.

Mary Ellen snapped out of her trance. She turned and trampled out the door and down the stairs. I was right behind her.

The loud opera music led us straight to Dr. Barney in the living room. He was facing away from us, conducting in his white sweater and tan pants. His arm swung wide. His yellow drink spilled on the carpet.

"Dad!" shouted Mary Ellen. "Dad!"

He couldn't hear us over the shrieking lady on the record. Mary Ellen didn't move.

I touched Dr. Barney's back.

He jumped and turned on me.

"Jesus fucking Christ!" he shouted. "What?"

I shouted back. "Arnie stabbed himself in the chest with your hunting knife!"

"My son knows how to handle a knife!" he bellowed. "Oh, I get it! This is a trick or treat thing!"

"No, sir," I shouted. "He's bleeding up there in his room right now!"

"You'd better be telling the truth," he said, "because I don't have a sense of humor."

We knew that.

"Yes, sir," I said.

Dr. Barney put down his drink and went up the stairs. When he got to the landing, he looked down. "I'm serious. I don't like games!" He turned and walked into Arnie's room.

Mary Ellen's legs went out from under her. She landed butt hard on the first step.

I took her hand. It was damp.

"Your Dad will patch him up fine," I said.

"God, I hope so," she whispered.

Her lips were pinched. She stared at the front door. Dr. Barney charged out of Arnie's bedroom and down the stairs. We got out of his way just in time. He had blood on his hands. The opera lady was shrieking.

We followed Dr. Barney down the hallway into the kitchen. A sob stuck in my chest.

"Victoria!" Dr. Barney roared at Mrs. Barney's back.

Mrs. Barney jumped and turned so quickly she nearly knocked the bowl of steaming red spaghetti off the counter. Her eyes went wide and scared, looking at Dr. Barney. I knew Mary Ellen was afraid of her dad. But Mrs. Barney was a grown-up. Her forehead hatched wrinkles like cracks on a hard- boiled egg.

"Robert, is that your blood?" she said.

"Victoria, stop overreacting," said Dr. Barney. "Go upstairs and deal with your son."

Mrs. Barney made a weird little sound. She took off her apron and folded it.

"One thing after another with your idiot son!" said Dr. Barney, scrubbing his bloody hands like he was angry at the bar of soap.

Mrs. Barney watched him for a second and then ran out of the kitchen.

Dr. Barney dried his hands and shoved the bowl of Mrs. Barney's steaming red spaghetti into the refrigerator. I'd been looking forward to her spaghetti all afternoon.

Dr. Barney wiped his sweaty forehead with the dish towel.

"Girls, how would you like a treat?" he said.

We heard a scream, like the opera lady, only louder up in Arnie's room.

"All right, girls," Dr. Barney said. "A treat it is."

He took a big bowl of fresh strawberries out of the refrigerator, along with an angel food cake that looked yellow in the fridge light.

Mrs. Barney came back down. She stopped at the kitchen door. Her dress had Arnie's blood on the front. We were close enough to hug her.

"The ambulance is coming, Robert," she said.

Dr. Barney cleaned strawberries like it was surgery.

"I called them too. Keep pressing that bandage," said Dr. Barney.

Mrs. Barney pulled at her red fingers. She took a small step into the kitchen, like she was scared to get too close to him.

"You're the doctor." Her voice was like splinters. "For God's sakes, he's your son!"

Mary Ellen threw herself at her mother and hugged her, blood and all.

Mrs. Barney gently shoved Mary Ellen back. "Honey, oh, honey," she said.

She ran back down the hallway, almost bumping into the walls.

"Mary Ellen," said Dr. Barney. "Put an apron on and help me."

Mary Ellen picked up her mother's folded apron and put it over her Tinker Bell tutu. Dr. Barney handed her a small knife.

Mary Ellen was moving stiff, like a robot. I wanted to get out of there. I wanted to take her with me. I didn't know what to do. So, I sat at the kitchen table and watched.

Dr. Barney was knife-twisting through the strawberries. Mary Ellen was trying to keep up, but her fingers kept slipping. The house got silent all of a sudden. The opera lady had stopped. The record was over.

But then the quiet got filled up again. An ambulance siren in the distance.

Mary Ellen looked at me. And then back at her fingers.

The ambulance got louder and closer.

Mary Ellen stopped slicing.

The siren was on our street. Then it was right outside. The loud high pitch filled the house and went right through me. Mary Ellen and I ran down the hall.

Mrs. Barney swung the door wide and let in the two ambulance men. They followed her upstairs, hauling a long stretcher.

The front door was wide open. It was dark out. Red ambulance lights flashed on skeletons, ballerinas, tiny cowboys holding big bags of candy.

Sounds came from Arnie's room that I'd never heard from Arnie's room before. The ambulance drivers carried him down on the stretcher and bumped the wall only once.

Mrs. Barney held on to the banister and was right behind them.

Arnie looked up at the ceiling. His body was covered in a white sheet with red blood stains.

"Mommy," he said. He looked so pale.

"I'm right here, sweetheart," said Mrs. Barney.

She grabbed her purse and keys and followed them out.

Mary Ellen and I went out on the porch and watched Arnie get loaded into the ambulance.

Some grown-ups and kids in the crowd held their ears as the ambulance roared away, red lights flashing, siren blasting. I wanted to go home.

"Mary Ellen!" Dr. Barney's voice boomed from the kitchen.

"Coming!" she shouted. "You can't leave me," she whispered and grabbed my arm.

Hells bells!

We went back into the kitchen. I sat down at the breakfast table again, feeling numb. Dr. Barney and Mary Ellen cut more strawberries. What were they making, a friggin' wedding cake?

The wall clock ticked. I spilled salt on the Formica table and made a design with my pinky. Mary Ellen washed her hands, took off her apron and sat across from me. I could see her mother's cracked-egg wrinkles starting on her forehead.

Dr. Barney served us the angel food cake topped with a huge pile of strawberries and whipped cream. I tried not to look at the blood on his sleeves as he sat down with us. My first bite cut right through a hunger I didn't know I had. Sun-ripe strawberries, soft white cake. The sweetness took my mind off Arnie. I licked the plate until all I could taste was my own spit.

Mary Ellen just sat there staring at the cake.

"Eat up, Mary Ellen," said Dr. Barney. He slid the plate closer to her.

Mary Ellen picked up her fork.

Dr. Barney looked over at me and said, "You licked your plate like a dog, young lady. I won't tell your parents. But I'll show you something sweeter than strawberries."

Mary Ellen wide-eyed me from across the table. There was a message in her face. I didn't know what it was.

Dr. Barney slid out of his chair and knelt next to me like he was proposing marriage. He leaned so close I smelled the yellow booze on his breath.

"This is called a butterfly kiss," he said.

His eyelashes fluttered against my cheek. Quick, quivery, and soft. The tickle of Dr. Barney's lashes turned wet. His eyes closed and his face pressed against my cheek. Then his shoulders rose and shook. I couldn't believe a grown-up man was having a crying fit on my face.

Across the table, I saw the quick nod of Mary Ellen's head toward the back door, telling me I could go.

Dr. Barney's big body shook. I pushed past him. He didn't fight me.

I got to the door, but it was locked.

Mary Ellen sprung up and unlatched it. She gave me a soft shove and I was outside. The coolness of the night felt damp on my Peter Pan tights. I looked back through the porch window.

Dr. Barney was pulling himself up off his knee, wiping his eyes. He picked up our plates and carried them to the sink. Mary Ellen ran out of the kitchen, taking her strawberry knife with her.

I jumped off the back porch, ran around to the front lawn, and headed straight home. I passed trick-or-treaters straggling across the street.

When I got home, Mother was giving out Halloween candy to a bunch of little vampires in black capes.

"What was all that hullabaloo with the ambulance?" said Mother.

"Arnie stabbed himself with his dad's knife, by mistake," I said.

"Dumb dad," said Mother. "Dumb kid."

She turned off the porch light. Halloween was over at our house.

Mother and I watched the Ed Sullivan Show. Bing Crosby sang "Swinging on a Star." Sid Caesar was a riot. Acrobats built a shaky human pyramid. I took in everything and tried hard not to think.

Mary Ellen called early the next morning, asking for a sleepover at my house. She wanted to come right away.

When she walked in the door Mother and I both said at the same time, "How's Arnie?"

Mary Ellen shrugged. "He won't die."

She said she just wanted to sit in my room and read magazines and listen to music. We didn't talk at all. I had questions, but I kept them to myself.

Mother didn't have any answers when things went wrong with kids. But sweets never hurt. So, she filled the house with a buttery cinnamon smell, baking her famous noodle kugel with two cups of brown sugar.

I ate, but Mary Ellen didn't.

Mother didn't know that Mary Ellen got sugar all the time over at her house. Even when she didn't want it.

CHAPTER 10
HORMONE CITY

Puberty! Maybe we should just freeze them until it's over.
—Mother

Bakersfield, June 1956

I sat alone in the top of our maple tree. Leaves rustled in a dry language. Shadows spread slowly across the neighborhood. The sunset was blood red.

All I had to do was jump and the awful pain would be gone. Being dead, I wouldn't care.

I mean, what the hell? I used to be the fastest, toughest kid in the neighborhood. I left guys in the dust. They called me Speedy Gonzales, like the cartoon.

How had those same buddies turned into Popeye overnight? Muscles rising like shiny loaves in the oven heat of Bakersfield. Dark hair massed in their armpits, voices creaking like gates in a horror film. Now, if I ran out for a pass, they'd tackle me, grab my chest, and stay on top way too long.

There wasn't much to grab. I was still the same: straight up and down. I loved my skinny, wiry, fast boy-body. I prayed every night that my tit bumps wouldn't grow blobby and fat like some of the other girls. When they ran, their whole chest bounced. Yuk.

When I complained to Mother about all the changes, she said, "For one thing, you're *supposed* to let the boys catch you."

"You said good girls play hard to get," I said.

"*Hard*," said Mother. "Not *impossible*. Understand, that if you want boys to like you, they get to be faster and smarter. Which are the preliminary calisthenics for getting one of them to marry you."

"I don't want a husband who's slower than me," I said. "Then I'd have to pretend to lose all the time." Besides, losing was like dying.

I asked Daddy if I was a freak. He took my boney wrist between his fingers.

"You're maturing a bit slowly for a girl of twelve. When you get older, you'll be grateful to look younger than your peers. Just keep on enjoying your childhood, sweetheart."

Childhood?

Even Tommy was in on the conspiracy. Our deal had always been that when he pissed me off, I'd chased him, catch him, and beat the crap out of him. He never bruised. Despite everything I did to him, he loved me. I think he might have even died for me. I probably could have counted on that, like some loyal dog.

But just today, when I lost my temper over a book he borrowed, I started after him. He didn't turn around and run away like he was supposed to. He just stood there and looked *down* at me. When did he get so tall? When had his curly blond hair turned brown? His eyebrows were now black and nearly ate his forehead. His fat gut had sucked into broad shoulders. And vengeance boomed in his curse. The old sweetness had fused into a horrifying snarl as he reached for me with hands as big as catcher's mitts. I ran like hell, through the house, into the yard, and up the tree. Thank God, the kid was no climber.

A hot breeze dried my tears. The maple branch held my trembling body. Jumping would be so easy. Vertigo didn't bother me anymore. I leaned forward and looked at the grass below.

"Dinner!" yelled Mother, from the back door.

A little careless, but not enough to die, I left the sunset where it was, and climbed down.

I followed the whiff of broiled steak to the kitchen table. Daddy was home for dinner for the first time this week. He looked so tired. He told us he'd done a long operation on a crop duster pilot who ran his Piper plane into some power lines and nearly killed himself. I thought, *What a spectacular way to die!* Electrocuted by power lines in an exploding Piper. I'd have to keep that in mind if I ever got serious about suicide.

Mother cut into her steak and started reading from *Time* magazine about the Korean War. Her teeth chewed into the words. I couldn't eat.

"Stop playing with your food!" said Mother, with an impatient glare.

Wow. It must've been a bad day for her too, because she closed *Time* magazine, and began filling our dinner time with a list of my stellar trespasses from birth.

"And when you were five you completely ignored my. . . and at seven you neglected to. . . and only this year you were still oblivious to. . ." Mother concluded with: "I'm pointing out a behavioral pattern here. It's your way of being, your responses to the world that are unacceptable in normal society."

What the hell was her problem? I was just being me. How could I *not* be me?

Across the table, Tommy pushed his food around the dinner plate too. His knee jiggled under the kitchen table. I could feel it on the floor and see it in his fork. He looked like he wanted to bolt out of there. Whatever was going on with him, he got to arguing with Mother about the Korean War. Then he cursed, threw his napkin on the plate and ran out. We heard his door slam. It felt like the whole world shook.

Mother picked Tommy's rumpled napkin off his steak and looked across the table at Daddy.

"This is going to be a bruiser," said Mother. "The two of them going through puberty at the same time. Maybe we should just freeze them until it's over."

Daddy smiled. He reached over and patted my hand.

"It's fine, sweetheart," he said. "You two are just entering the complicated years."

Seemed to me everyone was getting pretty complicated.

After dinner and a hurry-up dish washing, I went outside and did my nightly snail stomp. Mother paid a penny a pelt for what she called *justifiable carnage.* Crushing the little beasts that were eating her new plants. I was up forty-five cents this week.

After cleaning the goo off my sneakers, I walked over to Mary Ellen's house. Thank God, her father's car wasn't there. Dr. Barney was too weird.

I snuck past their kitchen window and saw Mrs. Barney by herself washing dishes. Which meant Mary Ellen was probably hanging out under the backyard willow. I was glad because I really needed to talk. We made sense of things together.

I scooted through the tangled path of blackberry bushes to the willow.

Mary Ellen's candlelight flickered through the drape of branches. It was a kind of fairytale hut at night. Dark limbs and small green leaves hung to the grass and hid us from grown-ups. Sometimes it felt more like home than home. In the afternoon, after school, we'd lay on our soft mats, suck hard candy, and paste the latest magazine cutouts in our Eddie Fisher scrapbook. Although Mary Ellen wasn't as happy with Eddie since he married Debbie Reynolds. She explained to me what a man does to his wife on their honeymoon. Gross stuff. She said she hoped Eddie didn't leave his thing inside Debbie all night because that destroyed a woman's insides. How the heck did she know all this stuff?

I started toward the draping branches. Mary Ellen's nasal laugh burst from inside the willow. She'd probably gotten a new comic. I had a *Tarzan* for her, but lately she'd been more into Archie and Veronica. Then, I heard a boy's deep voice. That sound twisted my gut. We'd never let a stranger in. The two of us had signed a blood oath on the place. Shadows moved inside the willow. Then a smacking sound, like someone eating ice cream loud.

"Ew!" squealed Mary Ellen.

Jesus! I pushed through the branches.

She was flat on her back. A boy was on top of her. The two of them sat up quick in the candlelight. Light and dark, arms and legs moving.

"Christ!" said Mary Ellen. "You should knock first!"

"Knock?" I said. "It's a tree!"

"Oh, grow up!" she said. "Can't you see I'm busy?"

"Hey, this is my place too!" I said.

"Since when?" she said.

That hurt.

The boy in khaki shorts moved his long legs. His face shifted into the candlelight. I couldn't breathe. Mel Ganz, from the basketball team. How the heck did a popular guy like him end up on top of Mary Ellen? Mel didn't look happy to see me either.

"Hi, Mel," I said. "What are you doing here?"

He dropped his frown and nodded toward Mary Ellen with a big grin. She fluttered her eyelashes at him. Yuk. A new draft on the candlelight brightened her body. I got a good look at her cut-offs. They were tight as pigskin on a football. A new blouse. Scooped neck. Not one we'd picked out together. And her nipples stuck up under the stretched cloth. The way he stared at her. I had to admit, it was hard to ignore those bumps.

"How'd you get out of the house looking like that?" I said.

Will you stop asking questions and get out of here"?" she said.

Mel slid his hand around Mary Ellen's waist and tilted his head up at me.

"See you later, alligator," he said, in a real snarky voice.

Then he leaned over and nibbled Mary Ellen's neck. She took in a quick breath and trembled. I felt that nibble. I felt that tremble. Mary Ellen's eyes were closed. Her bare legs, his long hairy legs rubbing each other like best friends. What I wouldn't give to dive right in among them.

My brain said leave. But my body said, STAY! This is like Eddie Fisher!

Watching Mel touching Mary Ellen, it lit a fire where I'd never had a fire before. The pleasure on Mary Ellen's face as Mel ran his hand up her thigh toward her privates. Holy shit! I almost crumpled from the shock in my shorts.

"MARY ELLEN!" Her mother's voice was the loudest on the block.

"WHAT?" Mary Ellen's voice was second loudest on the block.

"Homework!"

"Later!"

"NOW!"

"Damnit!" said Mary Ellen.

Wow. She swore in front of a boy.

"You still here?" she said to me.

Mary Ellen pulled on a sweatshirt and baggy pedal pushers that covered up her sexy outfit. So, *that's* how she got out of the house dressed like that.

"Tomorrow night?" she said.

"I'll have to think about it," I said. I knew she meant Mel.

"You're an idiot!" she hollered at me.

"You're the idiot!" I shouted back.

"I'll see you real soon, Mary Ellen," said Mel.

"You go on home now," she said to me. "Mel's mine."

Mary Ellen spread the branches and sashayed toward the house. I never saw hips sway like that except in Marilyn Monroe movies.

Mel smoothed the front of his khaki shorts. Those two rubbing together under the branches had stirred something powerful in the air. He spit on his fingers and fizzed out the candle flame. He was in a hurry to leave and so was I. We pushed out of the canopy together and into the moonlight.

"How the heck did you meet her?" I said, walking behind him.

"Ran into her at the Rexall," said Mel. "Bought her a Coke."

It was so simple. But that kind of thing never happened to me. I would always be on the outside looking in at everyone else's fun. I hated them.

In the front yard I nearly tripped over a football like a clumsy doofus. Mary Ellen's brother Arnie left his crap all over the place. I kicked the ball back toward the house and Mel picked it up. He stood with the ball like he was waiting for something. I raised my hands.

"Toss it," I said.

He looked at me, snickered, and passed the football underhand. Like for a girl.

I backed up and returned it hard, right at his khaki shorts. He caught it, looked a little surprised, and grinned a beautiful smile. He zapped the ball bullet-style at my chest.

I caught it solid and felt the full force of that thrust in every part of my body.

I threw the ball back and held out my hands for his return.

"Harder," I said to him. "Throw it harder."

CHAPTER 11
CHRISTMAS SHOPLIFTING

Check your watch!
—Mother

Bakersfield, December 1957

I was scared shitless of Christmas ever since Mary Ellen and Rolly and I started stealing. Well, not *stealing*. *Liberating*. We called ourselves the Literati Liberators.

Our holiday mission was to free hardcover *New York Times* best-sellers from the shelves of Mr. Hennessey's Book Store. Then we'd give the books to each other as Christmas presents.

With just five shoplifting days left, we gathered to plan the Literati Heist. Ducking cobwebs in Rolly's garage, we sunk onto pillows around the candle flickering in a dusty wine bottle. Mary Ellen leaned back dramatically on the pillows like a film star in her black tights. She held her Chesterfield in a long cigarette holder. Rolly adjusted his dark beret.

He'd drawn a small moustache on his upper lip. I wore my black turtleneck sweater from two Halloweens ago. Our literary pretensions included imitating the coolness of the Beatniks. We wrote poetry and read it to each other with jazz records playing in the background. We listened to wounded words of outrage in Allen Ginsberg's *Howl.* We read *On the Road* by Jack Kerouac and fantasized about hopping a freighter to Mexico. Being an intellectual in Bakersfield was our best revenge, and as close to social rebellion as we could get.

But, to my everlasting shame, I was on parole in the Literati. I still hadn't been able to actually steal a book. Last year I got as far as the door of Hennessey's. Then the ghostly image of Mother's disappointed face rose in my mind.

Rolly and Mary Ellen's disdain was easier to live with than Mother's outrage if I were caught. And so, I had turned back from the exit at Hennessey's and paid for *The Last Hurrah* that I had pledged to steal for Rolly.

What a disgrace I was.

"Look, I want you to succeed this year," said Rolly, in his kindest voice. "Try to understand that to steal for others is an act of selflessness. After all, we risk humiliation, family outrage, and jail time to simply give a gift to a friend. It is our humanity that we are reclaiming. An intellectual rebellion against society's materialism and greed, which is the wisest message of the Beats."

Rolly's words sounded true and ridiculous at the same time. And yet, being one of the Literati was where I belonged. It made me feel special. And not stealing made me a chicken shit in the estimation of my best friends.

"Not to put too fine a point on it," said Rolly, "but if you don't engage in the sacred ritual of selflessness this Christmas, you're out of the Literati."

I felt nauseous. Expulsion!

"Time for the crime," said Mary Ellen. She blew her cigarette smoke at the wavering candle flame. "Rolly, I choose you to liberate the newly published *Doctor Zhivago* by Boris Pasternak for me. My choice, because I love that the hero is a doctor and a poet. Now, what do you want me to liberate for you, Miss Yellow Belly?"

"I choose you, Mary Ellen, to liberate *Exodus* by Leon Uris," I said. "My choice, because I want to read about Jews winning for once. What can I steal for you, Mr. Rolly?"

Rolly patted my knee. "You, my love, must pilfer *Lolita* by Vladimir Nabokov for *moi*. My choice, because I love unreliable narrators. In this case he's a middle-aged literature professor who is obsessed with a twelve-year-old girl. And not in a good way. Why are you staring at me?"

I was horrified. "Why would you want to read that?"

"Because the *New York Times Book Review* calls it repulsive," said Rolly. "Obviously, it's an adult content book, which means that since you are under eighteen, you can't purchase it. This time, my love, you really do have to steal the book."

Oh, shit.

"Gotcha!" beamed Rolly. "Are you all right? You look ill."

Mary Ellen and Rolly laughed as they got up and brushed the dust off their clothes.

"See you after school tomorrow at Hennessey's," said Mary Ellen.

"Can't wait," said Rolly, and blew out the candle.

Walking home, I couldn't get my panicked heart under control. Breathe. Breathe. Rolly and Mary Ellen had gotten away with their thefts. No arrests. No convictions. No familial disgrace. If they could do it, I could too.

"Take her to Alcatraz!" shouted Mr. Hennessey in my nightmare. I didn't get a wink of sleep all night.

At school I was a complete wreck—no idea what the homework assignments were.

I kept reminding myself that I didn't have to do this. There was still time to back out. Just don't show up at the bookstore.

After classes, in a kind of brain-dead trance, I took the bus to Hennessey's and arrived early. The windows were painted with snowy Christmas scenes. Scorched holiday decorations swayed in the hot wind and rustling tinsel hung over the street. I sat on the bus bench and reached into my purse for *Rolly's Official Guide to Successful Shoplifting*. Perhaps a review of these typewritten sheets would help.

Rule One:
In preparation: Carry one schoolbook
on top of your binder into the store.

Before I could read further, Rolly and Mary Ellen descended from the bus. They had their schoolbooks on top of their binders. Camouflage in plain sight.

Rolly kissed me lightly on the cheek. "You ready? Show me your poker face."

I stood up and let my face sag.

"You look like a stroke victim," said Mary Ellen.

A passing car horn honked. I nearly jumped out of my shoes. Holy shit! It was Mother.

She waved as she drove by and pulled into a parking space a few cars down.

I looked at Mary Ellen and Rolly, who were looking at me.

"Suck it up," said Mary Ellen.

Mother strode up, looking spectacular in her new black-and-white dress with matching heels.

"Hi, kids," said Mother. She meant me. "Listen, I'm going to buy some scarves for the bridge gals. Meet me at the car in half an hour. We'll go pick out a Christmas tree together. Won't that be fun? You kids headed to Hennessey's?"

"Uh, yeah," I said.

"See you there," said Mother. "Half an hour. Check your watch."

Mother took off quick in her high heels.

If she said a half hour, she meant twenty-nine minutes. Would I ever be master of my own sorry fate?

Rolly put his arm around me. "My dear, we all work better under pressure."

"Check your watch, kiddo," said Mary Ellen. "You've got a dreadline."

"Dreadline, very funny," I said. Twenty-eight minutes before my arrest.

Rule Two:
Enter calmly and avoid
calling attention to yourself.

I followed the consummate thieves into the serenity of Hennessey's. Ah, the quiet. The pale blue walls, shelves of colorful spines, and comfy pastel chairs. The hush of a bookstore was different from enforced library silence. I always got into a kind of trance in a bookstore. Friendly titles whispered, "Choose me."

Rule Three:
Note the location of the staff and shoppers.

Old Mr. Hennessey was at the counter. Thick glasses. Thick volume in his gnarly hands. Queen Anne, his fat black cat, chewed on a paper clip.

In the overstuffed chair, a young mother read to her little girl.

An old lady browsed cookbooks.

Everyone was in their own little world. A perfect setup.

Rule Four:
Move to your objective slowly.

I headed into the stacked shelves, slowly, looking for *Lolita. L* for *Lolita*. Nope. *N* for Nabokov. No luck. *V* for Vladimir. *P* for pedophile. I was out of options. I surveyed all the tables and found nothing.

Then I saw the problem. Right behind Mr. Hennessey were copies of *Lolita* on a special shelf. The sign read, *Must be eighteen to purchase.*

There was no way to steal with Mr. Hennessey sitting there. Even the Literati couldn't fault me for that. I was off the hook! Though there was a small chance of using Rule Five:

Rule Five:
Create a diversion if needed.
Tripping, fainting, farting, throwing up.

But Mary Ellen had disappeared into the shelves. Rolly had sauntered to the table where *Doctor Zhivago* hardcovers were stacked. He laid his binder on the table, leafed through *Zhivago*, and put it on top of his math book. He picked up the binder and books, clutched them to his chest, looked around as though he hadn't found what he wanted, sighed, waved to Mr. Hennessey, and sauntered slowly out the door. Bravo! Rolly had just executed a perfect Rule Six.

Rule Six.
Put the chosen book on top of your own book and binder and clutch them to your chest.

Mary Ellen strolled out of the stacks clutching her binder and books to her chest. I assumed my *Exodus* was resting against her beating heart.

"You have ten minutes left," she whispered.

"There's no way I can steal the book with Mr. Hennessey sitting there," I whispered.

Mary Ellen gestured with her chin toward the counter. I turned slowly. Mr. Hennessey was gone. Was he in the bathroom? With his old kidneys, he could be there a while.

Mary Ellen headed for the front door. I was on my own.

Jesus. Nine minutes left. I hurried to the counter. Queen Anne purred at me. Did I hear a toilet flushing?

Lolita. There were ten books on the special shelf.

I moved to the end of the counter, dropped my binder and math book on the floor, and squatted as though to pick them up. No one seemed to notice. I scooted on all fours behind the counter. A few short lunges and I was under the *Lolitas*. It couldn't be this easy. I held my breath and reached up, expecting Mr. Hennessey to return any second. I grabbed a *Lolita* and retreated backward to the end of the counter where I'd left my binder and math book. I slipped *Lolita* under the math book. With both books on the binder, I stood up and crushed them against my wildly beating heart.

"Stop, thief!" is what I expected. But there was only an excess of silence. I was breathing so hard I could've filled a zeppelin. This was awful. This was thrilling. This wasn't over.

I suddenly realized I should have put *Lolita* on top of the math book, not the bottom. If I were caught, it would look much more suspicious, like not absent-minded, but deliberately stealing. What the hell was I thinking? Because *Lolita* was restricted, if I were caught, it was all over anyway.

Calm, calm. I had to control my growing panic.

Rule Seven:
Never bolt straight out the door fast
like a guilty person.

I took several deep breaths and patted my money pocket.

Rule Eight:
Always carry more than enough money to purchase your heist.
If caught, apologize profusely and pay.
Grown-ups want to believe kids are not evil, so let them.

I sighed, like I was bored, and slowly headed for the door and freedom.

"Come back and see us soon," said a voice.

I turned and saw Mr. Hennessy's son Hank. Where had he come from? Hank helped on weekends, which this was not. Hank with sharp blue eyes was on duty. The way he tilted his blond head at me. Like a warning? *Come back and pay, you thief.* What did he see in my face? I was so muddled I wanted to die. I smiled, stiff with fear, and charged through the door.

The only alarm to go off was in my head. Had I gotten away with it? The blood of victory pumped so hard it could have shot out my eyes.

Mary Ellen and Rolly were waiting at the bus bench. They were grinning, like I'd just lost my virginity.

"Finally," said Mary Ellen. "I figured they nabbed you."

I couldn't believe I'd gotten away with it. I had such a sense of accomplishment. And confusion. It shouldn't be this easy to be bad.

"I did it," I whispered.

Rolly kissed my cheek. "You did it well, darling."

The unbearable weight of the book terrified me. I slipped it into my purse. The tension began to drain. My pulse jogged back to normal. But the crime had left a putrid taste.

"Look out," said Mary Ellen, without moving her lips.

She smiled and waved at someone behind me.

Mother came toward us with a white shopping bag brimming.

"See you later, alligator," said Mary Ellen.

She and Rolly said good-bye to Mother and got on the bus as it was pulling up to the curb.

"Well, did you find anything you liked?" Mother said to me, full of smiles. She must have gotten some great bargains.

"Not really," I said. "I didn't buy anything."

"Oh, you must!" she said. "We have to support the only decent bookstore in this backwater. Tell you what. I'll buy you a hardcover for Christmas. Whatever you want."

No! No! No! Mother swept me back through the door to the scene of the crime. Mr. Hennessey and Hank greeted her sweetly, as they always did.

"Pick something juicy," said Mother with a laugh.

I turned around and walked quickly into the first aisle, A-F.

B for Bibles caught my eye. I checked out the sight line to Mother and Mr. Hennessey and pulled *Lolita* out of my purse. I quickly stuffed her behind a fancy hardcover Old Testament. Whoever pulled that Bible off the shelf would find themselves eye to eye with *Lolita*. How she got there would forever remain a mystery among the Hennesseys.

With *Lolita* out of my purse, I was swamped with relief. I wasn't a thief anymore. But now, without *Lolita,* I was out of the Literati. That really gnawed.

I tried to focus on picking out Mother's gift to me. I needed something benign, well-reviewed, and intellectually stimulating. Something that showed off my wide-ranging interest in the world at large. Mother would approve and we'd be chatting over the merit of my choice on the drive home. That would be lovely. A classic was a safe choice. As I turned to the A's, Jane Austen's *Pride and Prejudice* glowed in a gold-and-brown hardcover. I slipped her into my arms.

But the call of the wild Literati still beckoned. Rolly and Mary Ellen were always pushing me to some screaming brink. That's what friends were for. But I didn't have topple over the edge this time. I realized my decision for a crimeless life was still tenuous. I circled back to the Bibles. I pushed the Old Testament aside and stared at *Lolita*.

To be a thief or not to be a thief—that was the question. Who was I going to be? I could still slip her back into my purse. But there was no going back after this.

I hesitated, holding my breath.

I held *Pride and Prejudice* in one hand and *Lolita* in the other as though I were weighing them. Austen and Nabokov's weight was no longer equal. I knew damned well what was right. Fuck all, I said to myself. I couldn't handle the stinging guilt of robbing a sweet old man.

I tucked Jane Austen under my arm, composed my face, took a deep breath, and stepped out of the aisle, still half expecting to be handcuffed. I held up *Lolita*.

"Hey, Mr. Hennessey," I said. "Look what I found in the As."

CHAPTER 12
SPACEMAN BLUES

Marriage is your Carnegie Hall.
—Mother

Bakersfield, February 1958

I could barely breathe. The bathroom was heavy with preparatory odors: stringent Aqua Net hair spray, Revlon nail polish and the infantile scent of talcum powder. I choked and fanned the air as Mother sprayed my body with her Paris perfume.

In the mirror, my God, my hair. Mother's salon guy had flipped the dark locks like ski runs on either side of my head and frozen them solid with Aqua Net. I looked like a long-eared alien. Like my hair, I too had become trapped, subdued, and unresponsive to any natural breeze.

"Here comes more scaffolding," said Mother.

"Why are you making such a big deal?" I said, squirming. "It's just Willard."

"Just this once," Mother sighed, "let me enjoy having a daughter."

Her knuckles dug into my back as she fastened the push-up bra with pointed falsies that looked like lace cannons. I tracked her in the full-length mirror cinching a bright white garter belt around my waist. She cut off the price tag. There was already a pile on the counter.

Mother handed me white cotton gloves.

"Isn't this a little formal?" I said.

She showed me how to stick my white-gloved hands into the silky, flesh-colored stockings and pull them over my toes without a run in them. This was followed by her softly clipping the nylons to my garter belt.

I felt like I was being built from spare parts like the Bride of Frankenstein.

Mother zipped the metal teeth of the pink dress up my spine. It had a gray poodle sewn onto the front.

We were in the home stretch, and it was brutal. I pulled up the stiff-layered, scratchy crinoline half-slips to make the dress stick out perky. The gray poodle was nearly horizontal.

"Sit down on the toilet seat," said Mother, "and put on the heels before you ruin your stockings."

Sitting on crinoline was like sitting on barbed wire. I slipped my feet into the pink high heels, stood, and grabbed the countertop before I tipped too far forward.

"I'm worried," I said. "What do I say to Willard for a whole evening? We've never talked much."

"What does he like to do?" said Mother.

She made me turn toward her and powdered my eyelids Elizabeth Taylor blue.

"He likes to run," I said.

Mother sighed.

Willard Skooter ran like Mercury, with wings on his heels. He was a goofy-looking sophomore with stiff brown hair and the start of a receding hairline. We met one morning on the way to school waiting for the freight train to pass. I was perfectly content not to get any closer to higher education for as long as possible. My strongest urge was to jump into one those rusted boxcars. Ah, the freedom of those clicking wheels. Give me the hobo life!

Willard was counting rusty boxcars out loud, and after the caboose went by, he hollered, "Race ya?"

Now, every day after a quick lunch, we sped through the quad and onto the track. We pushed our lungs to bursting in the baking air. I always won. He didn't seem to care. I could love him just for that.

Mother stroked black eyeliner across my lids.

"You never have to worry about talking to men," she said. "They do all the talking. They think it's their job to entertain us. All you have to do is listen, nod, and laugh. LNL. Say it."

"LNL," I said. "But what if I have something to say?"

"Be brief," said Mother. "Just don't be disappointed when his eyes glaze over."

"What if *my* eyes glaze over?" I said. I could be as bored as the next guy.

Mother blew on my eyelids to dry the eyeliner. Her warm breath smelled like coffee.

"If you start to drift off," she said, "look into his right eye, and then his left eye. Back and forth. You'll seem alert."

"What happens if he stops talking?" I said.

"You ask him a question about himself," said Mother. "The sound of your own voice will revive you. And when he's finished one of his stories, you say, 'Really? Did you really?' Like you're impressed. That keeps them going forever. And remember the reward at the end of the evening."

"A kiss?" I said.

"No!" she said. "You get to come home and relax in blessed silence."

"Is this how you got Daddy?" I asked.

Mother smiled and rolled strawberry glaze lipstick on my mouth. It tasted sweet.

We stood side by side looking in the mirror. Mother slipped her arm around my waist. She tilted her head at our reflection.

"What do you think?" she said.

"Does it matter?" I said.

Mother's eyes got soft. "You really are at the pinnacle of your beauty."

At fifteen? This was as good as I got? I looked like a pink umbrella on high heels. If I were up any higher, I'd plunge headfirst into the bathtub.

Poor Mother. She was really enjoying her first attempt to turn me into every man's dream, propel me on the road to romance, and fatten the calf for the slow slaughter of married life.

I was already exhausted.

Mother was elated.

Pulsing with rare sentiment, she took off her gold necklace with pearls and fastened it around my neck.

"Your father gave this to me," she said. Her eyes moistened.

I was horrified. "Stop!" I said. "What if I lose it?"

"Don't come home," she said.

The doorbell rang.

"Right on time," said Mother. "Good. That shows he's eager. You keep them eager by showing reluctance." She patted my pink shoulder. "Practice. Practice. Marriage is your Carnegie Hall."

Jesus Christ! It felt like this was all happening without me. I knew Willard didn't care how I looked anyhow. I was always hot and sweaty by the time we drank our Cokes after the run.

Mother started out of the bathroom to answer the door.

"Wait!" I said. "I'm not ready!"

I felt like Eisenhower was leaving the war room, and D-day was up to me.

"What do I do?" I said.

She looked at me, deadly sweet. "You're my appendage. Don't do anything I wouldn't do."

She disappeared.

I'd show her appendage! I unsnapped the necklace and laid it carefully on the counter where she would find it. I wasn't going to worry about the damned thing all night.

I heard her open the front door.

"Willard, please come in," she said in her company voice.

Touching the wall for support, I took it slowly down the hallway.

This was a high heel nightmare for me. What sadist invented this dating misery? And what had Willard done to get ready? Change his underwear?

The front room was softly lit, like a movie set. Mother stood by the lamp that made her look young. Her interior designer was from Hollywood's old days.

The biggest surprise was Willard. He looked so un-Willard that I thought he'd sent someone else. He wore a nice brown jacket. A white shirt with a thin tie. Tan pants instead of his scruffy Levi's, and jet-black loafers. Even his dark hair was slicked down and shiny. It made his head look smaller, and brand-new.

Willard stared like he was trying to figure out who I was.

He laughed. "You look so. . .gosh, I mean, good." He straight-armed me with a gardenia corsage inside a clear plastic box. "This is for you."

I didn't move. These heels could catch on the soft rug.

"Willard, how nice," said Mother. "Let me help you."

Mother took the box from him and opened it. The powerful gardenia scent was like spilled perfume. She held the corsage's rubber wristband open as I slid my hand in. Mother leaned close and whispered. "Where's my necklace?"

I nodded toward the bathroom. She gave me that there-you-go-again-resisting-my-best-effort look. I already felt guilty, and I hadn't even gotten out the front door.

"Have her back at ten please, Willard," said Mother. "Oh, wait. You've forgotten something."

I hustled us to the front door, but Mother caught me and strapped her precious necklace around my neck. If it had been a two-ton elephant, I couldn't have felt more burdened.

Willard followed me out of the air-conditioned house into the evening heat. I guess he could tell I was a little wobbly on my heels because he offered his arm. A David Niven moment. I'd never felt so girly in my life.

Willard even opened the passenger door of the car for me. It was a beautiful green-and-white Caddy, shiny from a wax job. The inside smelled so clean. When Willard hopped in the driver's seat, I got a strong whiff of his Old Spice.

"My dad's car," he said. Like I couldn't guess.

He turned on the air conditioning. It hummed lightly. A cold shaft of air hit me on the forehead. We drove down Spruce Street and out of the suburbs. Willard flipped on the radio.

"*Rock, rock, rock 'til broad daylight . . .*"

"Bill Haley and the Comets," said Willard turning the radio louder. "My first forty-five."

"Mine too!" I shouted over the familiar lyrics.

We sang along until the song ended. Who knew? We had something in common besides running.

"How about that guy Elvis?" Willard said turning down the sound. He's asking my opinion? I get to talk! This wasn't in Mother's scenario.

"I don't care if his hips have been banned in Bakersfield," I said. "I like his music. Do you?"

He nodded and smiled over at me. I picked at the wrist corsage, waiting for him to start talking endlessly about himself. But he just hummed to the music. We rode without a word down the main street of Chester Avenue. I began to sweat. He wasn't acting according to Mother's rules. I wondered if I'd done something wrong.

Willard parked near the Rexall Drugs on the corner. He took my hand and swung it as we walked along the sidewalk. I felt like Debbie Reynolds and Eddie Fisher headed for a duet. Except no one in their right mind strolled for pleasure in downtown Bakersfield. The barren sidewalks were monster hot way into the night. The heat seeped right through my thin soles. At least I'd stopped walking at a forward angle. But talk about onions and bunions! The pointy shoe pinch was excruciating.

Willard stopped in front of Fedway Department Store. It was famous for having the first escalator in town. It only went up one story, to the furniture department, but it attracted a lot of passengers.

I saw my reflection in Fedway's plate-glass window over a white mannequin in a bathing suit. Mother's necklace sparkled around my neck. I touched it to make sure it was secure.

Willard grinned into the mirror image of us.

"I'll bet people think we're the handsomest couple they ever saw," he said.

"Willard," I said. "No one is paying the slightest bit of attention to us."

"Oh, sure they are," said Willard.

He turned as an older couple was walking into Fedway.

"Hot enough for ya?" he said. The standard Bakersfield greeting.

The older man tipped his cowboy hat.

"How about this heat?" Willard shouted as the couple hurried through the door.

My big toes were ready to fall off. The corsage had wilted.

"Willard, what are we doing?" I said.

"Showing you off," said Willard. "My mother, before she got sick, liked taking walks, showing me off. But no one looked at me because she was so beautiful."

"I think I've been shown off enough," I said. "I need to sit down."

In those heels, I barely made it back to the car. Without a word, Willard started driving.

"Willard, where are we going?" I said.

"A party," he said. "You'll see."

Well, at least there would be other people to talk to.

Quicker than spit, we were in the boonies. I didn't know where he was headed. We shot past Dell's Drive-In movie. A giant screen surrounded by a tall green fence. Kids were parked outside the fence in the field where there were no rules. Skinny bodies stretched out on the car hoods, kids drinking beer and making out.

We passed two gas stations, a bar, a small yellow plywood church, and a lot of swayback houses. Any further and we'd be in Pumpkin Center, where no one I knew ever went on purpose.

I was about ready to tell Willard to take me home. But he swung off the main road and parked the Caddy in front of a small two-story Spanish-style apartment building. A neon sign read: The Desert Arms. In front was brown grass, a dried-up fountain, and a few oleanders. I didn't see any party.

"Hey, Willard," I said. "What the heck is going on here?"

"No, no, it's OK," said Willard. "The party is upstairs, in my brother's apartment."

Willard looked too scared to lie. Going up the stairs in heels, I leaned on his arm until we got to the second floor. It looked deserted. But one apartment door was wide open. We walked slowly toward the sound of Pat Boone singing on a hi-fi.

"Love letters in the sand . . ."

Inside were college-age couples watching a replay of the Sputnik launch. The boys looked like Pat Boone with tan faces and light casual clothes. One guy even wore white bucks. The three girls had Sandra Dee haircuts. Jackets and tight skirts that were molded to their perfect thighs.

Willard and I were so far out of our league.

"Hot enough for you?" said Willard.

All the couples looked up at us and stared as we walked in.

One Sandra Dee said, "Lovely necklace."

I touched it. "Thanks," I said.

"Well, Willie," said white bucks. "Found a date, huh?" He strutted over. "Hi, I'm this bozo's brother. Call me Jed. How about a drink?" He winked. "Wanna try a martini like a big girl?"

"Sure," I said.

I wanted to punch his grin through his skull. Jed made me feel grown up and hopeless at the same time.

After introductions, Jed sat us on fold-out chairs. The crinolines cut into my legs so I focused on the girls who were doing Mother's formula. *Listen. Nod. Laugh.*

The guys were loving it. I had a lot to learn, but it didn't look like fun.

Willard and I were ignored, but the martini was fantastic. The liquid slid down my throat, cool and strong, and made my eyes water. Like drinking a pine tree with a green olive. I felt floaty from the first sip.

"Hey there," said Jed.

He'd been spouting off about Commies and came over to pour us another round.

"You know you're dating a future spaceman, right?" said Jed.

Willard's cheeks turned red.

"Willie here wants to get his rockets off. Right, Willie?" Jed snorted.

Everyone laughed but me. Willard downed that second martini in one gulp and stood up.

"We've got another party."

I barely had time to finish my martini before he steered me outside. I was feeling a little tipsy.

Jed shouted after us. "Hey, bozo, don't do anything I wouldn't do!"

Willard got me down the stairs and into the car so fast I nearly fell.

He grabbed a small pint bottle of booze from the glove compartment and chugged so hard his Adam's apple could've jogged loose.

I took a deep breath and closed my eyes, miles away from Willard's boozing. The drink had made me tired. What I wouldn't give to be lying in the hammock in my own backyard, dressed in shorts and a T-shirt.

Willard's sob made me sit up.

"I'm sorry," he said. "I shouldn't have brought you here. I wanted . . . well, since Mom died, I hoped me and Jed . . ."

Just as Mother predicted, Willard started talking non-stop. But not about himself. It was about his mother's slow horrible death from breast cancer. He'd race home from school every day, sit with her, read to her, and play her favorite Dean Martin records. She died with him holding her hand. I looked him in his right eye, then his left eye, trying to shut out his slur of words. That horrible picture of his Mother's death and Willard's own sad, lonely life.

I was never going to date again.

The dashboard clock read 9:30. Thank God!

"I'm sorry, Willard," I said. "But it's time to take me home."

Instead of starting the engine he scooted across the leather seat and threw his arms around me like a frightened kid. He kissed me on the mouth. His lips trembled against mine like a nervous little fish. My nose clogged from his booze breath and Old Spice.

I gasped, but Willard wrapped me tighter in his arms. I could feel Mother's necklace crimp against my neck. Our lips got chummier. Then I began to feel a kind of warm ache in my nethers, but it didn't take away from the crinolines scratching my thighs raw and the garter belt cutting into my waist. Willard moaned and rubbed his hard zipper against my poodle skirt. This must have been what Mary Ellen called the doggy rub. I gritted my teeth and thought of John Wayne.

"Ah!" Willard breathed out and threw himself back on the seat.

He pulled at his hitched-up pants. He was sweating and breathing hard like we'd been running. I felt for the necklace. It was still there.

"You kiss great," he said. "How many guys you kissed?"

"Just you," I said. "You're the first." I guess it was OK to admit that.

"Really?" he said. He sat up taller. Finally, I'd said something that made him happy.

"Yes, really," I said.

Really seemed to be one of those all-purpose words, just like Mother said. Oh my God. Mother! It was ten. I was going to get so grounded.

"Willard, I really have to get home!"

An apartment door slammed. The Pat Boones were on the move, laughing down the stairs.

"I don't want them to see us," said Willard.

Was he kidding? I looked back and saw Jed waving as our car spun out of the parking lot.

Willard got the car under control and whizzed us back to the suburbs. His face was lit up by the dashboard lights. I could imagine him on a rocket ship, machinery blinking.

That booze and the honkytonk Bakersfield sound on the radio was giving my brain a cozy buzz. I leaned back in the seat and watched the lights go by. I shed those awful shoes, stretched my toes, and remembered that armless girl on Cousin Herb's TV show who played the xylophone, holding the mallets with her toes. I dozed off dreaming of feet.

I woke up when Willard swung a hard right into my driveway. Every light inside and outside the house was blazing. The car clock said we were twenty minutes late.

I jammed my heels on and leapt out of the car without waiting for him to be a gentleman. The necklace! I felt for the necklace. Whew! I shook myself totally awake and headed for the house. Willard jumped out on his side and grabbed my arm as I went past.

"Wait! Look!" he said, pointing to the night sky.

I couldn't see anything until he came close and steered my head. Then I saw it too.

"Sputnik!" We watched the bright Soviet dot race past the stars.

"Someday I really will go into space," said Willard.

His voice was a little slurry. His clothes were rumpled. His hair had come loose from the slick stuff. He looked more like his old self.

"Would you like to come with me to the stars?" said Willard.

Now, that really was sweet.

"Anywhere but the Desert Arms," I said.

Willard's face broke into laughter. In all our days of running, I'd never see him laugh like that. The longer he laughed the less it sounded like laughter.

"Would you actually go out with me again?" he whispered.

"Hey, you two," shouted Mother. She was standing on the front porch. Her silhouette started down the walkway. "What are you up to?"

She was shameless.

Willard looked terrified as Mother came toward us.

I kicked off the heels again, reached under my dress, and wiggled out of the crinolines. A soft breeze caressed my poor chafed legs.

"Willard," I whispered. "Come on."

I turned and ran down the dark driveway into the street. The asphalt was warm. The rough surface tore up those clinging silk nylons.

Willard followed me, grinning.

I thought how I'd have to look Mother in the right eye and then the left eye and make up a good story. But right now, for the first time all night, my body was mine again.

It was just me and Willard. And Sputnik spinning our future overhead.

CHAPTER 13
RIDING HIGH

That girl is trouble.
—Mother

Bakersfield, March 1958

There's no shade in tennis.

One hundred and ten degrees on the court. Our bare thighs roasted on the flaking bleachers.

The team leaned into each loud *whap* of Killer Karen's swing. She was tied with Delano High's finest, a big-boned farm girl. If we won this last match, the Valley Championship was ours.

Karen's bronzed arm aced the ball hard enough to split a skull.

The farm girl spun a bullet right back.

Karen hit her famous spin sending it back over the net, just clearing the top. It hit the court and spun backward toward the net.

The farm girl ran like crazy for her shot, racket reaching. Her big head and shoulders crashed into the net.

WE WON! San Joaquin Valley High School champs!

Karen leapt the net, her peroxide ponytail a victory flag. She helped the red-faced farm girl up and shook her hand.

We all felt like whooping, jumping up and down, and pounding each other. But adhering to court etiquette, we clacked our rackets against the wood bleacher seats to make a polite machine-gun sound of congratulations.

Exhausted and hot, we brushed paint flakes off our tennis skirts and headed for the coach's Woodie station wagon. It had been a hard day. A hard play for all of us. These Delano girls were good.

I'd been the only one to lose my match, and I felt sick about it. The one good shot I made today was a one-with-the-universe wallop. I won a set point. For a freshman, I wasn't bad. But I had a long way to go to be as good as Karen.

We stuffed our gym bags inside the open back of the Woodie and headed for the Coke machine. My blood sugar was dropping faster than the fading sun and we still had a half-hour drive back to Bakersfield. I needed Stan's Drive-In treat that Coach had promised us. Free burgers and shakes if we won.

Karen strode over with her get-out-of my-way look. She didn't like backslapping or hooting her victories or even being touched.

"Good game, Karen," I said. I was ignored as usual.

She unscrewed her thermos of iced vodka and poured the Coke in. Usually, she just sipped after slicing up the other team. Today, for some reason she guzzled like she'd lost.

Her dad was the big drinker in her family. But Karen ran a close second.

Our coach and the Delano coach came up to us, hauling the trophy.

"Congratulations, champs!" they said.

We all crowded around to touch it. I took out my Brownie camera and their coach snapped our team grinning and holding up victory fingers. All except Karen, who was chugalugging behind the Woodie. Coach passed out Twinkies to go with our Cokes.

We called Coach the Frigidaire. Not to her face. But she really was unusually big and boxy.

"Hey Karen, big win today," said Coach. "It'll help when you turn pro." And then she added, "Now that you're finally graduating."

Coach shouldn't have teased her about graduating. Sure, Karen screwed up her grades cutting classes. But she was scary good at tennis. Timing and strength up the wazoo.

Karen ignored Coach, climbed in the back of the Woodie, and stretched her long body on top of our gym bags. Rosie, Reeba, Belle, and me crowded into the back seat. Big Sally sat her wide winner butt in front next to Coach, and Darlene Delaware got the window seat.

The big blue valley sky was turning purple. The Woodie cleared its lungs before sputtering out onto the highway. The dashboard clock read 6:00. We rode, half dozing, past flat dry fields that stretched all the way to the hazy Tehachapi mountains. A hot desert breeze blew across our salty skin and took away some of the sour smell of damp clothes, blood-blister socks, and orange antiseptic on torn-up knees.

I slumped against the seat with a good, drained feeling. Every muscle tuckered out. I let my mind drift, trying to figure where my game had gone wrong. A painful flick on my ear made me sit up. Karen was leaning over the backseat.

"Hey dog meat," she said. Her booze breath flooded my nose. "You were so bad today. You couldn't find a ball if it was swinging under a dick!"

That got a big laugh. She tried to flick my ears again.

I lurched forward. "Coach!"

"All right, you guys!" Coach shouted over the chugging Woodie. "Once a driller always a driller! Let's hear it for Bakersfield High!"

We yelled. "Drillers! Drillers! Yeah! Yeah! Yeah!"

Coach sang, and we all joined in. "A hundred bottles of beer on the wall, take one down, pass it around, ninety-nine bottles of beer on the wall . . ."

Karen laid back down on our gym bags. She was such a lawless frontier. Like Mother said, "That girl is trouble." But I always fell for people who made friendship a challenge.

The Woodie jerked and jolted. I looked over Coach's shoulder.

Plenty of gas, but we were losing speed. What the hell? It was always something with her car. Coach steered to the side of the highway just as the Woodie died. God, I needed another Twinkie.

"All right," said Coach. "We've been through this before."

It was so quiet without the chucking motor. A truck boomed past, spraying loose gravel, and the car shook. Fields darkening on either side of us were filled with oil wells that dwarfed the Woodie. They looked like a swarm of giant locusts that had just landed. Big metal heads seesawed up and down, probing the scrub.

"Take a break, team," said Coach. "I'll have the old girl sparking in a bit. She just needs to cool down."

She climbed out, pulling her wrinkled Bermuda shorts down from her crotch and hoisting the battered hood.

We scrambled out into the hot breeze and stretched our stiff muscles. Truckers caught us in their headlights and honked.

"Shit," said Karen. She grabbed her thermos and climbed out the back. "Why don't you just shoot the damned thing, Coach? I gotta to take a piss."

"Me too," I said.

Coach lifted her baseball cap and ran her fingers through her short curly hair.

"Don't go too far," she said, and handed Karen her flashlight. "Everybody who needs to go, follow Karen. The rest, join in here. A hundred bottle of beers on the wall. A hundred bottles of beer . . ."

Karen sprinted off toward the oil wells, leaving me, Rosie and Reeba without a flashlight. We followed Karen's jerky light ahead into the stand of creaking steel. A full moon cast rig-shadows on us. The sulfur smell got stronger as we moved past the grinding machinery. The air tasted bitter.

Karen was way ahead now, like she was off to seek her fortune in some distant land instead of looking for a place to piss.

"Where the hell is she going?" said Reeba.

"Not my problem," said Rosie.

"That girl's everybody's problem," said Reeba.

The three of us squatted behind different iron haunches. I heard their two streams hit the dirt. Maybe I could win something today. They finished, but my pissing was still going strong. Too bad there was no trophy for that.

"You musta drunk those hundred bottles of beers, squirty," shouted Reeba.

They laughed.

"Come on. Shake it off and let's go back," shouted Reeba. "This out here's giving me the creeps."

I met them in the moonlight.

"What about Karen?" I said.

We looked in her direction. She'd disappeared. A distant flashlight flickered high up.

Reeba squinted. "Christ Almighty! I think she's on top of a goddam oil well!"

"Let's go tell Coach!" said Rosie.

"You go," I said. "I'm going to make sure she doesn't do anything stupid."

"You mean stupider," said Rosie.

The two of them turned to go.

"Come on back with us," said Reeba. "She ain't never gonna like you."

A blush hit me. I didn't know my hero worship showed. Did the whole team know how I felt about Karen?

"You go on," I said.

The two of them took off. Probably laughing at me. But this was the last chance to hang out with Karen before she graduated, and her career took her over, and I never got to see her again.

I started walking toward her light, high in a rig. I felt like a midget surrounded by giants. My bare legs felt so naked. Then her light disappeared.

"KAREN?" I shouted.

Karen's voice came from the sky behind me.

"Hey, dog meat!" Her voice was slurred. "What the hell you doing?"

I whirled around and got her sudden beam in my eyes.

"Well, we're going to be leaving soon," I shouted over the creaking machinery.

"Right," she said. "By now they're singin' 'White Coral Bells.'"

I shuffled backward until I could see her white tennis dress small against the black sky and the huge shaft between her legs. How the hell had she gotten up there?

I took a good look at the two long metal legs making a pyramid up to the beam where Karen was. Jesus! She was about twenty feet in the air. The beam pumped up and down like a lazy playground seesaw. A motor was attached to one end of the beam by cables that powered the whole thing up and down. On the other end was the locust-headed looking tool probing for oil. I still couldn't see how the hell she made that climb.

Karen's body tilted. She looked like a rodeo queen conquering a slow-motion bronco.

"Come on up, dog meat!" she shouted.

Her flashlight beam lit up a crusty ladder on the side of the metal leg. All I had to do was start up to show her that I wasn't afraid.

"Hey, loser!" Karen shouted. "You know your big problem? You play like a girl!"

That was worst insult you could throw at someone on a girls' team.

I shouted back. "If *you* can make it up there, asshole, anyone can!"

I prayed Coach would be here any minute to tell me not to do what I had to do.

The ladder rung was filthy and slippery, covered in grit and oil. I felt the rig's vibration in my grip, in my whole body. At each rung I paused on the thin metal ladder and looked toward the highway. Where the hell was Coach?

"Coach ain't gonna save you," said Karen.

Shit. She knew how to pile on the shame.

A train threw a distant whistle into the stir of the night. That sound turned into the jerky pump of a car horn.

Damn. Why was Coach still back at the Woodie banging the horn? I needed her here.

From the top of the oil well, Karen hollered a rodeo, "Yeeeehaaw!"

Fear stretched that ladder to the stars. My sneakers felt slippery. Mother would kill me if she saw me doing anything this stupid. I didn't have to prove anything to Karen. Screw this. I was going back down.

I let my foot dangle and tried to find the rung below. The tip of my sneaker slipped. I grabbed. Caught the ladder. My ribs smacked metal. I yelled, barely holding on for the pain.

"Come on, dog meat," said Karen. She sounded nicer all of a sudden. "You can do it."

Maybe she heard my moan. I looked down. A tide-pull on my stomach. God, I hoped my vertigo wasn't coming back.

Oh, what the hell! I started climbing again. Legs shaking. Fist over fist. My eyes stung blind from sweat. I blinked, and then blinked again to clear the view. Karen was just a few feet away, her knees straddling the beam, her body tipping toward me.

Jesus! I'd made it.

"It don't get no better than this, dog meat," said Karen. "Get on board. We gotta date with the moon!"

That huge metal shaft she was riding sliced downward a few inches from my fingers. Christ!

"You ain't never been as bad as you were today," she said, with that same nice voice. "But you could be fucking good with a shitload of practice."

I was too stunned to say thank you. Karen's eyes turned dark and glittery.

"You know when you hit the ball just right?" she said. "That full feeling?"

"Yeah," I said. "Everything is perfect, for that second."

"Yeah, yeah," she said, and sighed. "Only time I feel whole."

"You'll feel whole all the time when you go pro," I said.

"You don't know a damned thing," said Karen, looking straight up into the night sky. The moon showed damp on her skin. "That kind of thing ain't for people like me."

"What people like you?" I said.

She stared like I was stupid. "People like me, dog meat. People like me, and my fucking dad."

Her dad? What did that asshole have to do with anything? He'd bought a used pickup a few months ago and had been driving himself into the drunk tank every weekend. He killed Karen's younger sister in the last crash. I was going to ask, what the hell did he have to do with her gearing up for Wimbledon? But Karen sat up straight and waved into the night.

"Well, hellooo, Coach!" shouted Karen.

Thank God. Coach was here. Her flashlight spotted the way.

My ribs ached so bad. I couldn't tell if it was me or the machinery trembling.

"Come on down, champ," said Coach. Her voice was tired. "We gotta go home."

Karen didn't move. But I felt for the rung below and got down quick. Dirt never felt so good under my Keds. Karen pulled the flashlight out of her jacket pocket, turned it on and tossed it high into the air. It landed and burst near Coach. We both jumped.

Karen leaned back and howled like a wild animal trapped in the moonlight. Her sound came from a place so hurt it nearly killed me.

A month after her graduation, on a hot Bakersfield night with the moon full, Karen got drunk and parked her dad's used pickup on the railroad tracks. If she was going for payback, she could've just killed his truck. When the train came, I wondered if Karen was howling at the moon.

CHAPTER 14
UNCIVIL WAR

Let's start over.
—Mother

Bakersfield, August 1959

"You're sixteen, right?" said Dr. Big Shot. "To have an ulcer at your age is very unusual."

He was tall and skinny and had pock scars on his chin.

"What's causing you such great anxiety?" he asked.

I'd known him all my life, but I didn't dare tell him that the tension between me and Mother had grown so thick you couldn't slice it with a Scandinavian ax.

My jaw was tight. My teeth ground at night. I stalked life with clenched fists. And then I got this tummy ache.

If my life depended on it, I couldn't say exactly why I was so angry at Mother. No way to pull apart the intricate weave of our discontent with each other. It just felt like she was a festering succubus inside my head. And I resented her make-your-life-a-gem advice, which I heard as, "You're too dumb to function on your own."

All I said to Dr. Big Shot was, "Do something for my stomach. It's killing me."

"Take this acid suppressor," he said. "Oh, and change your philosophy of life."

Philosophy? I'm supposed to have a philosophy?

The next week, Mother took me to another doctor, a specialist. Mother thought there had to be something deeply wrong with my brain since I never agreed with her. The specialist asked me a lot of questions and gave me a written test. When I was all done, he retreated to his office. Finally, he called us in with the results.

"Madame, your child is normal," said the specialist. "And very well-informed."

In my opinion, Mother was the one who needed a brain test. She'd probably fried her frontal lobes trying to control the universe.

Big Shot's acid suppressor worked. I could finally get some sleep. And, I tried out a philosophy. Every time I wanted to strangle Mother into silence, I'd tell myself, *Hey, she's an old lady who's lost her mind. Agree with her and then secretly do things your own way.*

I didn't maintain that for long. There was something in me that had to fight back. If I didn't fight back, I felt like I'd be devoured.

To keep my stomach calm and to get away from Mother, Willard and I would pedal to the Kern River, sit in the sand, and inhale the heat. But, just as soon as my wheels rolled back into our driveway, my body tensed for battle.

I think Mother and I both knew that if something didn't change soon, there was going to be a big A-bomb explosion in our house.

"We need a break," said Mother. "How about you spend your sophomore year at this top boarding school I found for you? It's in the Bay Area."

"When do I leave?" I said.

I almost felt like crying. Just the idea that I was getting away from her made the tension in my body melt. The Bay Area. I'd been born in Oakland. It would be like returning home.

"Just one thing," Mother said. "It's a *Catholic* high school, so you'll have to wear a uniform, and follow certain rules, and be normal. This will be a big change for you."

"Thanks," I nearly spat. "Are the nuns going to beat me?"

"Just don't tell them you're Jewish," she said.

Hell, after that ulcer, I could handle a few whacks from the nuns.

When school began, Mother drove me to the Bakersfield airport through the hot, tired streets that I couldn't wait to leave behind. Soon I would be able to breathe like a normal person without Mother's claws digging into my shoulder like some avian Poe misery. The deadly Bakersfield soap opera was over.

I was on an airplane OUT OF BAKERSFIELD! Bye-Bye!

The Palo Alto boarding school was a dark, old, two-story clap board building surrounded by century-old oaks. There were no nuns. The teachers were old ladies and the food was fattening, but the academics were incredibly challenging. I was stirred by those hunky gods in Greek mythology and their weird stories. Kill your father. Marry your mother. I mean, Mr. Oedipus, you weirdo!

My naughty nature began to slosh up against the boarding school's wall of well-established school rules. Our stupid uniforms were white sailor shirts, long navy-blue pleated wool skirts, and a tie the color of our class. Green for sophomores.

I refused to wear the uniform tie properly. Instead of letting it hang around my neck under the sailor collar, I wore it angled from my shoulder across my chest like a soldier. I was the rebel. I got regularly dinged. The other girls snickered their approval.

It was satisfying to see how far I could push the system here. I refused to go to the Stanford church on Sundays for services which was required by the school.

"Everyone has to go to church," said the principal.

"As a Jew, I reserve the right to worship with my own people."

Like I gave a shit.

But since Jews don't have services on Sunday, I was herded into the bus with everyone else. I had to admit, the Stanford Memorial Church was a beauty. But I couldn't relate to the sermons. I stared up at the stained-glass windows and made-up stories to keep my brain occupied for a couple hours. Why the hell was religion so popular when it was so boring?

While the boarding school was more entertaining than my Bakersfield boxing match with Mother, it was also like being in prison. Full-time boarders like me weren't allowed to leave the premises unless accompanied by a responsible adult. My roommate, Nadine, an overweight blond, had family in Marin and always disappeared on the weekends. I was the only one who didn't know someone on the outside. I'd sit on my bed and write sad letters to Willard, Mary Ellen, and Rolly. The window screens were so thick almost no light got through. I wandered the long halls of the dorm and ate my meals in the dining room with a few of the staff.

To get some oxygen in my brain, I jogged through the compound, past classrooms, dorms, infirmary, administration, and the gym.

I began to long for my bike Romeo and the Bakersfield freedom of pedaling anywhere I wanted to go under the sun.

The lifesaver was the camaraderie of my fellow boarders during the week. They too had been sent from troubled homes, so we easily coagulated into a team of inspired insurrectionists.

The greatest gift to our gang was the irresistible target of the British house mother. Miss Smith-Jones's thick body stood so invincibly straight that she didn't even look human. Her tailored tweed suit fit like a uniform. The dark-brown bun on top of her head was shiny, like a wet turd. She was older, maybe fifty.

At the beginning of the term, she gathered us for an introduction. Surveying our faces through thick glasses, she spoke without a pinch of humor.

"Ladies, I am new here too. I have spent my entire working life in the British boarding school system. I believe it is a great value to society to have girls raised properly. I will enforce strict rules of deportment. If you follow the regulations, we will get along. If not, infractions will be severely punished. I assume there are no questions."

Miss Smith-Jones turned quickly and walked back into her large room at the apex of our dorm hallways. She closed her door quietly. We were left standing there trying not to laugh.

Quite by accident, or rather *because* of an accident, I made an important discovery. One day, Mary, the Irish exchange student, cut her finger with my scissors, trying to even her bangs. I ran and knocked on Miss Smith-Jones's door.

"There's a bloody finger out here," I said, as she opened the door.

Her face turned white. Her chin trembled.

"How dare you!" she said.

"What?"

"Use that foul language! Go to your room."

"But Mary sliced her finger," I said.

Color returned to Miss Smith-Jones's face. "I beg your pardon. I will get my kit."

After that initial odd response, I realized that the old Brit thought *bloody* was a bad word. Naturally, I shared my discovery with the gang. We gathered in my room and practiced until we were ready to release our assault.

"Top of the *bloody* morning to you," said Mary, holding up her bandaged finger.

"Shame on you!" said Miss Smith-Jones.

At breakfast my roommate Nadine said, "Good *bloody* morning, Miss Smith-Jones."

Miss Smith-Jones cringed. "That's foul! Go to your room!"

After church I said, "Wasn't that a lovely *bloody* sermon today, Miss Smith-Jones?"

"Oh, my Lord!" said Miss Smith-Jones. "No lunch for you!"

After a few months of this mantra, poor Miss Smith-Jones realized that we were willing to endure whatever punishment she meted out just to watch her flinch. She sunk into a perpetual state of outrage, withdrew into her room, and barely spoke to us. Nevertheless, as the term progressed, we carried on with all kinds of irritating nonsense.

I organized one such incursion. To honor the death day of my favorite actor, James Dean, who was killed in a 1955 car crash, I led a memorial demonstration. I told everyone to dress as a ghost, with a sheet over their head, and parade after me down the long hall past Miss Smith-Jones's door chanting, "Bloody, bloody boy."

As we did, sounds came from behind her closed door. It may have been sobbing. We couldn't tell. But we rarely saw her after that, even at meals. As a result of her absence, we got away with more than we should have. Some girls even snuck out at night to meet with boys from the all-male schools nearby. I never had the nerve to go over the wall.

But, even with all our wonderful trespasses, I missed my old life. I was getting edgy and sad. Nothing could substitute for glorious freedom. I wanted to go home.

~

One night, I woke to the sound of a screaming ambulance siren that had stopped right outside the school. When I opened my door, there were loud voices coming up the stairs. I grabbed my robe and trotted down the hall where a crowd gathered at Miss Smith-Jones's door.

Two ambulance men trampled up to her room and went inside. A little later, they guided her down the stairs. She looked feeble and bent, a hundred years older than when she got here. She was twitching and crying, apparently in the full throes of a hysterical breakdown. At least that's what one teacher called it.

I was shocked. I didn't know kids could have such a horrible impact on adults. Sure, we'd been a bit rough on Miss Smith-Jones, but I thought that was our job. Good old-fashioned kid gouging. Mother would have shot me before she'd let me drive her that crazy. Why didn't Miss Smith-Jones know how to protect herself from a bunch of restless teens? As a seasoned housemother, she could have just changed her bloody philosophy of life.

The staff followed the ambulance men and Miss Smith-Jones down the stairs, murmuring. They glanced back at us with disgust.

It didn't exactly come as a surprise when our little gang was asked to remove ourselves from the school premises at the coming midterm, only a week away.

I began packing up and wondered what punishment awaited me in

Bakersfield. My stomach began to churn at the thought of Mother's reaction.

The upside was that I would soon be hugging Willard after all our lonely letters. Mary Ellen and Rolly would welcome me home. I'd be doing wheelies on Romeo under the bright-blue sky of Bakersfield.

When I got off the plane, my body soaked up the deep, searing heat. I felt strangely whole again. I wanted to twirl on the tarmac just to feel the desert's wide-open warmth.

Through teary eyes I saw Mother coming toward me. No hugs. I followed her to the gleaming car and put my suitcase in the trunk. A horrible tension simmered in my gut.

Mother drove in silence. Air-conditioning was on full chill. I glanced at her stern profile. That coiffed hair, that perfectly made-up face, that soft double chin.

I had missed Mother. I had missed Mother more than I knew I could. Had she missed me? Bad as we had been with each other, being with her felt so familiar, so family . . . ish.

After Mother parked in our driveway, she turned to me. Her face was almost friendly.

"Look," she said, "maybe the boarding school wasn't a good fit. Let's just start over."

Her tone seemed a little more careful now. I wouldn't go so far as to call it respectful.

"You behave," she said, "and get good grades, and I'll have a very big summer surprise for you. And I mean *big*. Think you can do that?"

So, it was all up to me?

"Let's *both* give it a try," I said.

CHAPTER 15
THE WALL

Religion is the worship of absurdities and atrocities.
—Mother

Bakersfield, June 1959

Returning to Bakersfield High after having been to a private school, the kids were a little in awe of me. One girl asked if I'd been sent away for an abortion, but everyone else was just curious to know what it was like.

Mary Ellen and Rolly were disappointed that I hadn't been beaten by nuns like in novels.

Willard kept hugging me like he thought I might pack up and leave again.

Compared to the tough academics of private school, Bakersfield High was so easy, I almost didn't have to study.

Even so, I couldn't forget the pale face of Miss Smith-Jones. What we had done to that old lady was a revelation, a new perspective on how fragile people were. Even grown-ups. I wondered about Mother. Her invincibility. I wondered what it would take to destroy her like we destroyed Miss Smith-Jones. And then I felt guilty for wondering.

When June finally rolled around and sophomore year was over, I brought home the best report card of my life. Mother was impressed. But she hadn't yet told me what the big surprise was. Until one day, she came home singing Cole Porter's, "I Love Paris."

She opened her purse and waved tickets at me with a huge grin on her face.

"Your big pay-off has arrived," she said. "Start packing!"

After all these years tethered in redneck central, Mother was finally going to Europe. On the *Liberté* no less. The famous French luxury liner was advertised as having excellent cuisine, fine wine, waiters with accents, and nightly shows.

Tommy refused to shop for the trip. But Mother and I tried on all the wash-and-wear dresses we could find in Fedway and Brock's.

"I wish someone had taken me on a trip like this when I was sixteen," said Mother.

I thought, *Jesus Christ, I really am one lucky son-of-a-bitch.*

The *Liberté* blew its massive horn and backed into the Atlantic.

I covered my ears and waved good-bye with my elbows. Daddy was on the dock, waving back. Sadly, we wouldn't see him again for weeks. Tommy and Mother tossed handfuls of confetti over the railing. I stood for the longest time watching Daddy and America slowly disappear into one long wet horizon.

The *Liberté* was not exactly geared for younger people. The food was great, but how much shuffleboard can you take? Tommy and I got in as much trouble as the boat had to offer. We snuck up to first-class where there were chandeliers. The first person we ran into was Dinah Shore. We scrambled up to her for an autograph and were asked to leave. She looked older than she did on TV.

It would be days before we docked in Le Havre, so Tommy abandoned me for the ship's library. Which was fine, because by then I'd met Latchme Nureem at a ping-pong tournament. He was an Indian diplomat from British Guiana. We were evenly matched, so we got to be best friends. It made Mother nervous that he was middle-aged and married, and that he asked me for every dance at the nightly band show. I was a skinny sixteen, but grown-up enough to flirt, even if this was my maiden voyage.

When we docked at Le Havre, Mother quickly got us off the liner and into a cab. By the time we arrived in Paris, it was like she'd had ten cups of espresso. All that pent-up energy from years in Bakersfield gushed into a non-stop marathon of touring. With a thick guide book and a map that unfolded forever, Mother led us through the Louvre, the Musée d'Orsay, the Grand Palais. We hopped on board a Batueaux-Mouche up the Seine and ended the day on top of the Eiffel Tower. I don't think we ever rested from sightseeing except to sleep and eat.

"Please hurry, *garçon*," said Mother. "We have a tour bus to catch."

Of course, the meals arrived in the leisurely European fashion, and it drove her nuts.

Poor Tommy said, "Can I just stay in the hotel and read today?"

"Absolutely not," said Mother. "Think how enriched your life will be after this."

In the hilltop district of Montmartre, I found my dream. This was Picasso and Dali's neighborhood! On every corner there were painters with easels. Tiny shops sold art. Cafés were filled with artists wearing paint-splattered shirts.

Someday I'd come back here, rent Picasso's garret and have an amazing painting career. The place lit me up. I was planning my future while Mother's hungry mind was devouring the past.

Mother smiled all the time now, making good jokes and trying out her own high school French with some success. Clearly, she felt at home here.

~

One afternoon we were strolling past designer shops. Mother stopped in front of a fancy glass door. The gold sign read: Yves Saint Laurent Haute Couture.

"This is where the high-end clothes we've seen are designed, displayed and sold on live models," said Mother. "Hey, Jan, just for fun, go in there and ask for a job as a model."

"Are you kidding?" I said. "I'm as straight up and down as a ten-year-old boy."

"Just see what happens," said Mother. "You'll have a new adventure. Remember, everything you do enriches . . ."

"Stop!" I said. "I'm going!"

Inside the Couture House everything was elegantly white and gold, and chic as hell. An impeccably dressed, tuxedoed man came toward me and asked me what I wanted.

"Mademoiselle, qu'est-ce que tu veux?"

"Je veux un travail de mannequin," I said.

He tried to hide his smile, and shook his head slowly. His slender hands made the air shape of a woman with breasts and hips and all the things I didn't have. He gestured to the gorgeous, tall women with amazing figures who gathered around us, looking my skinny boy figure up and down. They smiled and tittered when he told them why I had come.

"Au revoir, Mademoiselle," said the man, as I slinked out the glass door.

Mother greeted me with a smile. "So, how did it go?"

~

We made a huge dent in Mother's Paris list of "enriching adventures." Then, for variety, she had us bus from one small charming French village to another until we reached Strasbourg, a rustic town on the German border.

After a dinner of Wiener schnitzel, sauerkraut, and a crepe dessert, Mother and I sat by the huge fireplace with mugs of hot chocolate. Tommy was in his room with the new mystery by Patricia Highsmith, *Strangers on a Train.*

"Tomorrow we'll cross the border into Germany," said Mother.

"What! Are you kidding?" I said, slightly hysterical.

Germany was the epicenter of my lingering Holocaust fears. The war only ended fourteen years ago. I didn't want to see former Nazis driving cabs, selling pointy hats, serving poisoned apple strudel.

"Let's forget Germany," I said, "There's all of Europe."

"We're picking up a Mercedes in Stuttgart," said Mother. "It's a more flexible way to travel. We won't be subjected to other people's schedules."

We were just picking up a Mercedes? Well, that was impressive. I could get behind that idea.

Mother sipped her hot chocolate. Firelight flickered on our steaming mugs.

"You're happy here, aren't you?" I said. "You haven't harped at me once."

Mother turned to me, smiling.

"I was just thinking how much better behaved you are," she said.

I was terrified as the uniformed German border guard looked at our passports. His pale blue eyes snapped open and shut fast like a machine gun. I wanted to turn around and run back to Paris.

After a two-hour bus ride to Stuttgart, we took a taxi to the large Mercedes-Benz factory. Tommy finally put his book down. He seemed captivated by the car's design; the sleek blue exterior, the real leather seats, the burled wood, and the small innovations we'd never seen before.

I named the car Hans so he could feel part of the family. I remembered Grandma saying she'd never ride in a German car. Mother had obviously gotten past the Holocaust heaves.

"My plan is to drive to Munich," said Mother. "From there we'll go through Switzerland, Italy and then Madrid. That's where we'll meet up with Daddy."

"All that in ten days?" said Tommy. He looked exhausted.

The main problem with Hans was Mother. She loved stopping in the small, picturesque German villages on the way to Munich. But once the motor was off, she struggled to start it again. We got help from friendly locals. Nice as they were, they gave me the heebie-jeebies. Guys in lederhosen speaking their guttural German. German police car sirens made the same sound as when they came to round up the Jews in the movies. I pleaded with Mother.

"Please, let's get out of Germany," I said, "while we still can."

"Sure," said Mother. "But first I want to see a concentration camp."

"No!" Tommy and I chorused.

"Aren't you curious?" said Mother.

She drove us to Dachau.

We looked up at the huge, thick concentration camp walls. They were made of gray concrete that towered far above our heads. The oppressive height seemed to cut out the sounds from the town, as well as most of the sky. I held my breath walking through the gate.

A guard handed us a disclaimer. It said that the citizens of Dachau had no idea such atrocities were taking place in their lovely town. But that was such an obvious lie. Their vintage homes were built right up to the foot of that giant wall. They couldn't avoid seeing boxcars of Jews transported through the gates. And the smoke from the ovens filling the sky, as well as the putrid smell of burnt human flesh. What the hell did the town folk think the Nazis were doing? Those Dachau residents breathed the ash of us into their lungs. They washed us out of their brocade shirts. Now they wanted to deny their complicity.

I shook with anger as we crunched over a neat pebble path that led to the concentration camp museum. Inside the large rooms, giggling German schoolchildren pointed at the pictures of naked, skeletal bodies of starving Jews. The story was in bold type next to each exhibit:

> After days in the train boxcars, the Jews arrived at Dachau and were told they could have a shower. They were persuaded to undress and enter the bathhouse. Instead of water, lethal gas came out of the faucets. Gold was extracted from the corpses' teeth and sold for the value they contributed to the Nazi war effort.

One exhibit was baskets of Jews' teeth.

I wanted to strangle those happy German children. But at least they were awed to silence at the display of lampshades made from Jewish skin. Some of the lampshades had blue numbers on them, because Jews were tattooed when they entered the camps. Their numbers were written down in a book and their pictures were taken. Nazis could flip through the pages to find the face of the Jew whose skin was stretched into a lampshade that lit their home. Leave it to Nazi ingenuity to transform genocide into a craft.

We walked past the ovens. What an unholy sight. Thirty thousand humans burnt to bone. I noticed a heavy silence. No birds sang. I heard my own footsteps on the gravel like the thousands of footsteps murdered here. On the way back to the gate, there was a monument. It was metal and grotesque. The plaque read: Never Again.

Good luck with that.

We left in silence. There was no revenge in being a tourist. I felt guilty walking out of Dachau when so many had never left.

I had a deeper understanding now of why Grandma refused to ride in a car made with German hands. After Dachau, I knew where those hands had been.

I inhaled the light mountain air of Switzerland. The release of tension after Germany was intoxicating. I felt like I was floating amid the wide expanses of green meadows and tall white Alps. As we drove, Mother told us the legend of Danish King Christian X. During World War II, when the Nazis forced Jews to wear armbands, he wore an armband too. I renamed our car King Christian even though Mother said she didn't think the story was true.

Tommy remained stretched out in the backseat with a book. He was unresponsive to the changing landscape. When his eyes darted up from the pages, he looked dazed.

Mother continued to struggle with the mechanics of King Christian through Northern Italy. The countryside was so beautifully romantic, like a painting. The ancient villages with glorious churches, handsome people and great food made me want to hug everyone. I renamed the car Guido.

Mother was still having problems whenever we stopped Guido. Finally, at a gas station, her limited patience exploded.

"When we get to Spain, I'm selling the car!" she said. "Mercedes gave me a lemon!"

She renamed the car Citrus.

When we reached Madrid, Mother drove directly to a used car dealer. He inspected Citrus and said there was nothing wrong with him. That it had to be Mother's problem. She sold him anyway, at a loss.

"It was worth it," Mother sighed, as we taxied to the hotel.

Daddy had arrived and was waiting for us in the lobby with his sweet smile. I had never seen him anywhere but Bakersfield. I had to adjust my brain to make him real in a Madrid hotel.

He opened his arms, and I threw myself into them. His short-sleeve shirt felt soft and warm and familiar. I never wanted to let go.

That night we ate at the hotel restaurant and watched slim, angry dancers in black beat a terrible racket with their heels. The drama on their faces was so intense, like a dance of death.

In the morning Daddy was on the balcony with a cup of coffee watching the sunrise. His body looked so relaxed. In Bakersfield, I'd never seen him stand still. Without the pursuit of his daily routine, this is what Daddy looked like. Although, unlike Mother, he didn't look like he belonged.

Once again, the unquenchable curiosity of Mother led the family through endless museums, tours, historical sites, and nightly musical events. I watched Tommy and Daddy's eyes grow tired as they dragged after us. Poor guys. They longed for their private routines. Mother knew this about them, but she couldn't help herself. She was as addicted to adventure as Daddy was to work.

But finally, the guys had had enough.

"I want to go home with Dad," said Tommy.

Daddy was leaving in a couple of days and offered to take him back.

The desire to return to Bakersfield was inconceivable to me.

We hugged and said our good-byes at the airport. I could see the great relief in Tommy and Daddy's faces when they boarded the plane and flew home to where they truly belonged. I think Mother was relieved too. She stood up straighter and handed me my plane ticket to Israel.

~

Israel was just a concept to me, the place where Grandma's Zionist fundraising landed and part of my weekly allowance disappeared.

During our taxi ride from the airport to the heart of Jerusalem, I remembered what the family said every Passover. "May we celebrate next year in Jerusalem." I could just see Grandma kvelling over us being here, in the homeland she'd worked so hard to build.

Mother signed us into the famous King David Hotel. She didn't even want to take the time to unpack. After getting our key, we were soon strolling on the hot, busy sidewalk of Ben Yehuda Street, smiling at all the Jews.

Jerusalem wasn't a pretty town. The buildings were desert colors, dull sandstone or gray. But every inch of the place had a biblical story attached. And that made it breathtaking. I was walking in the footsteps of our Jewish ancestors, who ate matzah with Moses, survived the desert exile, and built this thriving town.

I suddenly realized my shoulders were relaxing in a way I'd never felt in Bakersfield. When Grandma called Israel a *homeland*, she really meant *home*. Everyone here was in our Jewish family. The taxi driver, that ice cream guy, all the politicians arguing in the Knesset.

Of course, that was delusional, as I soon found out. Not everyone here was Jewish. Almost every religion in the world claimed some part of this tiny country as their own. In the Old City, Mother and I wandered through gates that separated the Armenian, Jewish, Muslim, and Christian quarters. Roman Catholics shared the Holy Sepulcher with Greek, Coptic, Ethiopian, and Armenian sects. Everyone's history here dated back so many centuries that no one could successfully argue who had first dibs.

That night, Mother and I strayed into a square where people were folk dancing. In Bakersfield, Mother and Daddy square-danced, and this didn't look much different. Some of the young people around my age were dressed in army uniforms. They sipped espresso in the cafes with automatic rifles on their laps. It felt reassuring that the whole of Israel seemed armed and ready.

I talked with a few older Israelis who had survived the Holocaust. Their humor, laughter and conversations were aggressive, argumentative, and passionate. Not one of them agreed with the other about art, politics, or religion. They were tough. They had to be, to have survived the hell I'd seen at Dachau. I felt exalted to be among them. They were amazing. They were exhausting.

Even though Mother and I were assured that the Arab quarter of Jerusalem was safe, we had avoided exploring it. At the end of our stay, we finally girded our loins and headed for Damascus gate. The tiny shops were brightly lit and close together, forming a kind of colorful tunnel along the ancient streets. Some passages were so narrow that we could touch the walls on either side. We had just turned a corner when a young Arab boy saw us. He whipped out a gun, aimed it, and pulled the trigger.

"Bang! Bang!" he said.

We jumped back against the wall. The kid laughed hysterically.

Mother's face was white. My heart was pounding.

He came up and proudly showed us his toy gun. It looked real. It reminded me of my first John Wayne six-shooter.

The kid took Mother's arm and said something that sounded like, "I'm sorry."

Mother was still shaking. She and I sat down at the nearest Arab café and ordered a cup of thick Turkish coffee and baklava. Sugar and caffeine always pulled us back together again.

I watched the Arab kids play up and down the narrow street. I thought back on all the children I'd seen on the trip. Different languages. Different costumes. In the end, just kids. If grown-ups played with cap pistols too, the world might survive.

We had two days left before we had to go back to Bakersfield. I had to see a kibbutz after growing up with Grandma Bertha's tall tales of giant Israeli vegetables.

Mother and I took a bus tour to the countryside through fields and orchards, and were let off in front of the kibbutz's communal cafeteria. The air was desert hot. We were greeted by a young woman in shorts who showed us their whole setup with a distinct pride.

Everyone was engaged in some kind of work. Of course, there were no tractors sporting tires made of giant olives. Or roofs built from giant celery stalks. But I got a few laughs sharing Grandma's tall tales.

What I saw made a deep impression, the reality of what it took to feed this new nation. The courage, tenacity, and ingenuity of the kibbutzniks made the desert bloom against all odds. It seemed like a miracle. I guess that's why Israel's Prime Minister, David Ben-Gurion, said, "Anyone who doesn't believe in miracles is not a realist."

On our last day, Mother said, "I have to visit the Wailing Wall before we buzz back to Bakersfield."

"If we don't go back to Bakersfield, you won't have anything to wail about," I said.

She smiled as we ambled though passageways, markets and finally finding our way to a length of stairs. In front of us was a huge plaza, a football-field-sized square of flat stones. On the far side was the ancient wall where people were bowing, davening, and praying.

"Two thousand years, and the wall is still standing," said Mother. "The holiest site in Judaism, Islam, and Christianity."

We walked quickly across Prayer Plaza and stared up at sixty-five feet of history. The last time I looked up at a wall this big was Dachau.

I noticed a short wooden fence separating the women on our side from the men who were bowing and mumbling prayers on the other side.

I turned to an older woman standing close to me. She was writing on a piece of paper.

"What's up with the little fence?" I said.

She smiled. "The men say the scent of a woman distracts them from prayer. It's flattering to think my old body odor could get a man excited enough to forget his God."

She turned and stuffed a piece of paper in a crack between the wall's limestone blocks. I realized there were hundreds of paper scraps wadded into the seams. She handed me her pencil and a bit of torn paper.

"You can ask the wall for a wish or leave a prayer," she said. "Either way, don't hold your breath."

A cynic. I loved it. I smoothed the paper and tried to think of a good one.

Mother leaned over and whispered. "Look at them praying. Worshipping absurdities and atrocities. All this nonsense, for what? Religion will be the death of us all."

I'd never thought seriously about religion. But here in Jerusalem, it was layered on everything, like dust.

I heard a Rabbi here say, "Religious tradition is our structure for survival." A teacher once told me that a belief in something feels better than a belief in nothing. Grandma said her was religion was laughter.

I looked at the faces of the men and women who were praying their hearts out to a wall. They looked so deeply and beautifully absurd. I was glad that they got comfort and hope from their prayers. Because not everyone had it as easy as me and Mother. But really, we're all so momentary and miniscule, what difference does it make what anyone thinks? It's all good. That was my religion.

On the torn piece of paper, I finally wrote to the wall: *Call me.* I stuffed it in a crack.

When I returned the pencil, the older lady said, "Oh, by the way, you can send your prayers to the wall by telegram, too."

It was depressing climbing into an airplane that would soon deliver us back to Bakersfield. I felt the gentle pull of memories from the wide world we'd left behind. Mother and I slept as the plane roared over the Atlantic. When the morning sun streaked through the small window, I saw New York's silhouette that signaled we were half way home.

With a slight jolt, the airplane wheels lowered. Mother's nails tapped on her purse. Was that morse code for help? What would Mother do for stimulation without Europe outside her window?

She turned to me with her wild energy not yet tamped down in preparation for the Bakersfield backwater ahead of us.

"Did you have fun?" said Mother.

"I sure did!" I said.

"How about we do this every year? Somewhere new in the world, every year, you and me?" She said it like a ten-year-old conspirator.

All I could do was nod, profoundly grateful to be in on the game.

CHAPTER 16
THE SECRET PARTY

Stop hanging out with those drama kids!
—Mother

Bakersfield, December 1960

All us drama kids sat on the sidewalk and warmed our backsides against the cement wall of Harvey Auditorium.

I'd been sneezing all over my Virgin Mary robe. It felt good to take a break from the cold dust of backstage. Cars drove by and honked at us in our biblical costumes. End-of-day traffic on H Street.

Willard handed me a Camel and shoved his Joseph beard onto the top of his head. He lit our cigs with his flame-throwing Zippo and we inhaled together. He aimed his exhale at the shiny halo circling my head like the rings of Saturn.

Willard and I had been pinned for most of my junior year. I loved his deep brown eyes and receding hairline. I was always drawn to withdrawn guys like him. The ones who disappeared while you were talking to them. It was like being in the presence of something that had no real need of you. It worked for me.

I thought this Christmas pageant might bring us a little closer as Mary and Joseph, the dynamic duo. It turned into a nightmare for Willard. He didn't understand theater people at all, or why I loved my gang of wild, insecure, extroverted divas.

The stage door banged open. Mary Ellen stumbled out, wings shaking, white gown dragging on the sidewalk. She heaved into her usual bush. She picked a yellow piece of vomit off her glistening robe and flicked it at us.

"Look at my guts," said our dark-haired angel. "I got the whole goddam show on my shoulders. All you guys have to worry about is the manger consignment."

"But you're the star, Miss Monroe," I said, batting my eyes.

After graduation, Mary Ellen planned to head for New York's cold-water walk-ups with our gay buddy Rolly. They'd share rent, apply themselves relentlessly to auditions, become calloused against rejection, and anticipate sweet inevitable success. If all else failed, Mary Ellen planned to sleep her way to the top. Rolly said he was on board with anything that involved a penis.

What I planned was a more stable life in a Paris garret. I'd live on red wine, thick cheese, day-old baguettes, Gauloises cigarettes, and inspired French lovers. Like Picasso, my paintings would hang in the Louvre. I'd handle fame well. Mary Ellen and Rolly and I would meet up in New York at the height of our careers to celebrate our success and look back in wonder at our humble Bakersfield beginnings.

Actually, everyone in the Bakersfield High Drama Club was counting on their life being a challenging, tortured, short swim to the top. We all knew that to be a great artist, you had to claw your way up from the bottom of despair.

Now, our buddy Rolly had the perfect setup for suffering. The tension in his family was horrendous. His Dad was the studly high school football coach. His brother was the star quarterback. And Rolly was obviously gay.

My challenge was different, perhaps even more difficult. I had parents who hovered over me with embarrassing abundance. I loved it. I resented it. I counted on it.

Mary Ellen observed, in one of her theatrical outbursts, that I was "deficient in motivational misery."

I told Mother what Mary Ellen said, and added. "So, you and Daddy are making it very difficult for me to develop into a tortured, fabulously famous artist."

"There's plenty of artists who are successful without suffering," said Mother.

"Name one," I said.

"Norman Rockwell."

"Are you kidding?"

"Look," said Mother, "suffering for art is a myth. If you're smart, you'll observe the pain of others and avoid it. Just stop hanging out with those drama kids!"

Mother was famous in my book for missing the point. We misfits of Bakersfield High were a tightknit group. We were working collectively toward our tortured destinies. Depression and suicide were big topics at lunch.

Actually, I did have my private moments of despair, an honest *sad*, as we called it in the theater. After our productions, I never got invited to the gay kids cast party. Being left out was crushing. Rolly and Mary Ellen enjoyed all kinds of glorious bohemian excess. But Mary Ellen was straight too, so why did she get invited and not me?

I nearly jumped when the backstage door banged open again. Miss B, our drama teacher, stepped out of the doublewide door.

"Children, keep those cigarettes away from the costumes! Ten minutes to places." Her way of speaking bit into each word so clearly, she sounded British.

Miss B twirled back through the door. She was probably aware of how graceful she looked. We called her Miss Brillo-pad for her fender-streaked gray hair. It made her look a little like Frankenstein's bride. She also looked like a miniature Joan Crawford with those big-shouldered suits. Rumor had it that in her glory days she'd gotten frisky in the arms of Gene Kelly. Her life's passion now revolved around her sick mother, twelve healthy cats, and the best drama department in the state. She was completely dedicated to our lives of grown-up pretend. Probably more than any of us deserved.

We flipped our ciggies in the gutter and followed her into the dark backstage of the auditorium. It always smelled like dusty curtains and stale coffee.

Willard and I took our places on the slippery new manger hay and tried not to knock over the cardboard sheep.

"Tits up, girlfriend!" Rolly whispered to Willard as he passed us.

Rolly stroked his own dick and blew Willard a kiss.

I held on to Willard's trembling fist while Rolly morphed into a Charlton Heston-style narrator. Grasping the podium in his striped robe and gray wig, Rolly looked magnificent enough to part anyone's sea.

"Places, everyone," whispered Miss B.

She turned to the girl at the light board. "Trudy, lights."

The whole set turned crimson, as if we were bleeding from every pore.

"Trudy!" hissed Miss B.

Trudy corrected our skin tone to ancient sepia. Perfect. All the elements of our artificial world were in place. Miss B applauded silently. Audience noises swelled from the other side of the curtain.

Mary Ellen stood on top of the white bleachers above the choir, a static composition. Her wings and white robe were copied from a Renaissance painting. Heavenly light shone from above. Below, the fog machine swirled soft clouds at our feet. A tittering choir of twenty-five kids shifted in the tiered center of the stage, adjusting their purple robes and clearing their collective throats. Mary Ellen was doing her breathing exercise. I inhaled with her, as if that would help.

"Break a leg, children," whispered Miss B.

I hovered over our blessed little butterball with what I hoped was a maternal gaze. Willard loomed over the plaster cherub with a paternal slump. He shot me a look that said, *You owe me big time for this shit.*

The orchestra out front began their Yuletide welcome.

This was my favorite thespian moment: when the heavy red curtain rose, and the audience expelled an appreciative *ahhh.*

The student orchestra played as Mary Ellen and the chorus sang a schmaltzy medley. Christ's wise men ganged over to the manger and plopped down their gifts. The wow finish was when we all sang, "Silent Night" together, and Mary Ellen's voice led us toward a sweet crescendo.

The final applause was thunderous, and we took many undeserved bows. I never wanted it to end. I envied Mary Ellen. We both knew applause would follow her for the rest of her life.

The curtain was up, and families flocked on stage. Mother strode over with Tommy.

"A Christian halo on a Jewish princess," said Mother. "Only in Bakersfield."

Tommy snapped a black-and-white picture of Mother and me with his new Polaroid camera.

Willard's father gave him a back-thumping congratulations. Rolly's mother was all smiles. But his coach father never showed up to his gigs. Mary Ellen's mother was there, but not her nutty dad. Probably just as well.

At long last, the families funneled out of Harvey Auditorium into the warm evening air of Bakersfield.

In the crowded dressing room Mary Ellen sat in the chair next to mine, making no attempt to change into her street clothes.

"Stay in costume," she whispered.

We sat together until the last kid dashed out the door to the straight kids backstage cast party.

"OK," I said. "What up?"

"Follow me," said Mary Ellen.

Was she kidding? Miss B would kill anyone who didn't hang their costumes neatly on the rack.

Like an idiot, I followed Mary Ellen's long white gown out of the Harvey, into a warm December night and across the street to the parking lot. Shit! I forgot the damned halo was still on my head.

Rolly, also still in costume, was waiting in the driver's seat of his dad's Pontiac. He looked at me with a strange grin. Mary Ellen looked at me weird too.

"OK, you guys, what's going on?" I said. "It's not my birthday."

"You still want to go to the party that dare not speak its name?" said Rolly.

"What!" I couldn't believe what I'd just heard. "Me? Oh, you guys, you mean. . . ?"

Mary Ellen shoved me in the front seat between them and climbed in. I couldn't hug them because of the damned halo. But hell, I was going to the gay kids' party!

"Thank you, God!" I shouted.

"Oh, shut up," said Mary Ellen, grinning.

Willard pulled up next to us on his motor scooter. He glared silently at me through Rolly's open window. Oh crap! I was so excited about the gay party, I'd forgotten. This was payback night. He'd done the pageant for me, so I owed him the Stan's Drive-In special: A Giant Triple burger, a Double-Trouble milkshake, and Big Boy fries. Seconds if he wanted. I'd promised.

"Step on it, Rolly!" said Mary Ellen.

Rolly gunned the motor and burned rubber out of the parking lot. I looked back. Willard stood in a cloud of blue smoke, righteous fury on his face.

Oh, my God. I was so ashamed. And relieved. And ashamed to be relieved. I just folded my hands and looked down to get steady. How would I live with this? How could I face Willard?

Rolly burst into song and Mary Ellen followed.

"Bang, bang, bang, went the trolley . . ." They knew every musical on earth.

"Sing!" sang Mary Ellen.

I couldn't.

We drove through Bakersfield proper and up into a half-finished suburb overlooking the lights of the city. A dark purple sunset filled the sky. After a few twists and turns among half-finished homes, our headlights illuminated biblical figures cruising across the cul-de-sac toward an isolated ranch-style home. It looked like market day in Jerusalem. I recognized a few drama kids from East High, West High, and the junior college.

Rolly parked. We jumped out and followed the crowd. The front lawn manger figures were lit as only someone from a drama department could do. Sinatra's "All the Way" played from a speaker. At the door stood the most gorgeous movie-star-handsome man I'd ever seen. I could barely catch my breath. He was dressed in a white toga with gold leaves in his dark hair. Like us, he had on pancake make-up, eyeliner, rouge, and lipstick. He was older—maybe in his late twenties.

"This handsome devil is Howard," said Rolly. "Teaches drama at the college."

"Welcome, my sweet," said Howard to Rolly, and they hugged with a warm joy.

Howard took my hand. "Welcome, Mother Mary, you glorious Virgin."

He kissed my hand in a courtly manner, like Errol Flynn. No one had ever kissed my hand before. A warm tingle ran up my arm. I could be in love with Howard if I didn't know better.

Mary Ellen broke the spell by grabbing my arm and pulling me into the house. Heavy gold drapes shut out the night. Over Howard's slate fireplace was a startling life-sized painting of a nearly naked St. Sebastian. His torso was pierced by arrows, his face in ecstasy. Greek marble statues of nude men were lit up on fluted pedestals around the room. In genderless robes were a sea of girls with girls, boys with boys. The night floated on their sweet laughter. Mary Ellen leaned toward me. "When I come to Howard's, I feel like I'm coming home to the home I wish I had."

I looked back and saw Howard plant a deep kiss on Rolly's lips. I was surprised that it took my breath away. Gay love had been everywhere around me in drama club, but this was the first time I'd seen it for myself. Rolly's face, his shining love for Howard, and Howard's for him. I needed to adjust to this amazing new underworld. To breathe it in and make it real. What I needed was a moment alone.

"Where's the bathroom?" I said.

Mary Ellen seemed reluctant to take her hand off my shoulder.

"We need to talk," she said. "When you get done, find me."

Her eyes were urgent.

"Sure, fine," I said.

I strolled down the hallway, taking in the etchings of naked men beautifully framed on the wall. A blue bathroom door was open. Bruce, one of the wise men, had his robe pulled up to his frilly red underwear, a lathered leg on the tub, a razor in his hand.

"Need to pee, darling?" he said. "Go ahead. I'm almost finished. Can't do this at home."

I sat on the counter and breathed deeply. "I'll wait."

He smiled at me and pulled the razor slowly along his soapy shin.

"So, welcome, at last," he said.

I laughed. "Happy to be invited. Finally!"

"Yes, finally." Bruce winked.

"What?"

"Congrats. You and Mary Ellen."

"No, wait. Are you kidding?"

"You're here, aren't you?"

"Is that what she told you?"

Shit! Is *that* why she invited me?

I ran out of the bathroom and pushed through the crowd until I found Mary Ellen and Rolly in a room with gold-mirrored walls labeled *The Orgy Room*. They were sitting with Howard and a bunch of costumed kids crowded around a marble table. Liquor bottles were lined up on a giant Lazy Susan: Seagram's, bourbon, champagne, Scotch, sloe gin, vodka.

"Darling," said Howard. "Welcome to the mixed drinks marathon!"

I shoved in next to Mary Ellen and bumped her hard with my hip.

"You crossed the line," I said.

Her unfocused eyes told me she was well into the marathon.

"I wanna talk to you too," said Mary Ellen. "Except it's my turn."

Rolly poured her a shot glass of Jack Daniel's. Mary Ellen gargled the booze before she swallowed. Her eyes watered, and everyone laughed. Then she gave a speedy recitation: "If Peter Piper picked a peck of pickle peppers, how many peppers did Peter Piper prick?"

"Prick!" They all laughed again. "Prick!"

Mary Ellen's penalty was to sip another shot.

"I 'ove you," she murmured.

"Screw you," I whispered. I was sweating in my Virgin robe.

Howard leaned toward me. "You two OK?"

"They're fine," said Rolly. He handed me a shot glass of sloe gin. "You'll like this. It's sweet. Now drink up and then say the words fast."

I shoved back my wide sleeves and downed the booze. It was *too* sweet. I shuddered and said the words perfectly before the liquor hit my brain.

Howard smiled. "For a virgin competitor, you sounded very . . . experienced."

Wise guy. Everyone laughed and applauded. I couldn't confront Mary Ellen here. It was easier to keep drinking. As the game went on, chandeliers started multiplying above my head. Bombay Sapphire Gin, fizzy Moët champagne—you name it, we drank it. My face tobogganed into the mixed nuts. I had to get out of here.

I struggled up, mangled my way through robed bodies. Sweat slid down my pits. I followed a fresh chlorine breeze that wafted in from the backyard. A stunning patio with a fountain of carved fawns and fish, a kidney-shaped swimming pool with underwater lights. Golden calves of papier-mâché hung from trees, and colored garden lights splayed bovine shadows on the adobe fence. Everyone's robes rippled with a reflected glow from the pool. Couples swayed as Judy Garland sang, "You made me love you. I didn't want to do it . . . "

I'd never seen faces so intense, so focused, so happy. Their counterfeit selves were gone, if only for one night. All love was good here.

I flopped into an overstuffed lawn chair and shut my eyes. Had Mary Ellen loved me all the years we'd been best friends? She had boyfriends. I tried to remember if there were hints.

"Dance with me."

I opened my eyes.

Mary Ellen held out her hand. I struggled up and nearly tripped on my robe.

"You told everyone we're a couple?" I said.

She pulled me toward her. Her breasts bumped against mine. Weird.

"But we are." Her voice was unequivocal. "Friends for life."

"Yes, of course," I said. "But a *couple*? That's different."

"You're an idiot," she said.

Before I could call her an idiot, she swatted the halo off my head, lunged and planted a kiss on my mouth. The shock of her lips, her booze breath. I pushed her away.

"What the hell are you doing?" I said.

"What are *you* doing?" she said. "You knew!"

"I didn't," I said. "I didn't know. I'm sorry!"

Angry tears down her face. "I never should have invited you!"

She sobbed so hard, I thought she might fall. I had no idea what to do except hold her. She was dissolving into her gown.

There was a gentle touch on my shoulder.

"I'm so sorry, sweetheart," said Rolly. "She's been so . . . "

Mary Ellen's face rose off my chest. I've never seen such misery.

"I told my parents I'm gay," she said. "My father is kicking me out."

Ah, Jesus! *That's* where this came from! Then I wasn't her deepest sorrow.

"I told them I was in love with you," she said.

"What! They'll tell my parents *I'm* gay!"

She blinked tears at my horrified face. "No. No. They won't. They're too ashamed. Dad said people like me are sick. He's a doctor, he should know."

"Your Dad's insane," I said. "Why would you even listen to him?"

Dr. Barney was certifiable. How dare he call *her* sick!

"Mary Ellen," I said. "I know you better than anybody. Except I didn't know you were gay. But I do know you're not sick."

She grasped my arm with a terrified smile.

"So, we're still family, right?" she said. "You won't hold this against me?"

"Of course not," I said.

"But what do I do?" she said.

I had no answer. Rolly put his arm around both of us. Mary Ellen buried her face in his robe. Then just the two of them embraced. He nuzzled her hair.

"We'll get through it," said Rolly, "It's not like we haven't been through this crap before."

What crap had they been through before that I didn't know about? Why didn't they tell me? Watching Rolly and Mary Ellen hold each other so sweetly, I felt ashamed. I couldn't think of anything helpful. I was sure Mother wouldn't let her move in. What could I offer my best friend? I was such a shit. I bent down and picked up my halo.

"Where you going?" said Mary Ellen, wiping her eyes.

"I don't know," I said. "I'd like to go home."

"Lucky you," said Mary Ellen.

Ah, Jesus! I shouldn't have said *home*.

"For crissakes, I'm sorry," I said. "I'm sorry!"

I turned and staggered toward the house, away from her helplessness and mine. I still felt the blunt warmth of her mouth on mine, her body against my breasts. Inside, the house was too hot. The buzz of booze and sex was like a tidal wave. I had to get out of here, even if I had to walk home.

Howard was still conducting the mixed drinks marathon. He got up and came over.

"You OK?" he said. I guess I looked as bad as I felt.

He was so gorgeous, so kind. He put his arm around my shoulders. No wonder people came here. I let the tears out. Beautiful Howard. He held me for the longest time.

Another surge of young men and women, eager and loud, crowded through the front door. Howard let me go of me with a kiss and moved to greet them.

I pushed through their laughter, through the front door, and outside onto the grass. I looked up at the stars. Inhaling deeply made me even dizzier. I was flat on my back before I knew I'd fallen onto the soft cushion of Howard's front lawn. I felt weighted to the ground by the robe. Then all the lights disappeared.

Hands shook me awake. Slowly, I opened my eyes. A shadowy face hovered.

"You?" I said.

Willard gathered me in his arms. I held him close and breathed in his sweet Old Spice scent.

"I'm sorry," I said. "I'm so sorry."

He helped me onto the back of his motor scooter. I tightened my knees to keep the heavy robe away from his wheels.

"Willard . . . I'm really sorry," I said.

I wrapped my arms around his waist and put my cheek against the solid feel of his thin back.

"Tighter, lesbo," he said. "Hold on to that halo."

I smiled and kissed his shirt. Laughter and party lights faded as the scooter sped us along shadowed cliffs.

"Where do you want to go?" he said.

There was only one place I wanted to go.

"Home," I said.

CHAPTER 17
THE KENNEDYS COME TO BAKERSFIELD

Everything you do enriches your life.
—Mother

Bakersfield, September 1960

Finally, an evening to relax. Nothing was required of me. I leaned back on my bed, hiked up the pillow and got a country music station on the radio. That honky-tonk Bakersfield sound was strangely comforting with its simple heartbreak lyrics.

I flipped open our new *Time* magazine to catch up on the world.

Mother leaned in my doorway. "Get dressed. We've got a fundraiser tonight."

"Are you kidding?" I said. "You promised Tommy would do the next one."

"Your brother's a little impossible right now," said Mother. "Come on, get up. As you know, everything. . . "

". . . you do enriches your life," I said, finishing her sentence.

God almighty, I could quote this woman in my sleep.

Mother came in and put on her lipstick in my mirror. Why couldn't she use the mirror in her own room?

"Get it in gear," she said. "John Kennedy's going to be our next president. You'll be glad you met him."

"Teddy's brother?" I said. Teddy Kennedy, my gorgeous six-foot-two hero. "Why the heck didn't you say so? Is he as good-looking as Teddy?"

"Better," said Mother.

I jumped off the bed and dove into the closet for my new dress. I'd been daydreaming about Teddy since the fundraiser last month. He'd given a great speech that knocked me out.

"Elect my brother and change the world!" he'd said, with a Boston accent that sounded sexy on him.

Actually, it wasn't so much what he said. It was the way he looked. There was a ruddy glow about Teddy, like he'd been out catching passes in the sun. His shoulders filled out the dark suit and made it look too tight. He gave off something I couldn't see, but I could sure feel. And so could the other women. A Democratic chorus of sighs. We cheered him like maniacs.

Left to my own devices, I would've clawed my way onto his airplane, shouting, "Take me. Take me with you!"

One last look in the mirror. My new green silk dress was perfect, but too wrinkly across the boobs. I stuffed some balled-up nylons into the bra for an improved silhouette. Mother said beauty was persuasion, and I had some persuasion in mind. Just before we walked out the door, I grabbed my autograph book.

We were out of the air-conditioned house, and into Daddy's air-conditioned Cadillac with a half hour to spare. While Daddy drove and Mother adjusted her pearls, I relaxed in the backseat and opened my autograph book to Teddy's big scrawl: *We need your help. Teddy.*

He needed me.

I'd show John what Teddy had written. He'd put me in touch with the man of my dreams. This should be a cinch.

As the car sped through town, I closed my eyes, remembering the day after Teddy left Bakersfield. All lathered up, I'd biked to the downtown library and sat at the biggest table while the librarian slowly piled up newspapers and magazines.

> Born 1932, youngest of nine, his brother John was his godfather. Ted was a mediocre student.

I could relate. Who needs grades when you're the warlord for a national campaign?

I thumbed through *LOOK* magazine and found Teddy's picture at his childhood home in Hyannis Port. Mama Rose and Papa Joe were on the porch rockers, proudly watching their huge brood play tag football on the front lawn. All of them with the same toothy smile. I kissed Teddy's picture and imagined our engagement.

"Mother, Father," Teddy would say. "I'd like you to meet my fiancée."

Then I'd run out for a pass and catch it mid-jump. Score a high-stepping touchdown with his parents cheering. And if Teddy himself ran for office one day, I'd be right by his side, tackling soft-bellied Republicans who got in his way of making the world a better place.

The bad news was the picture of his blond wife. I eliminated her with an imagined headline: *Divorce Rocks Kennedys*. My plans moved on to our endless love. I already knew his touch from his massive warm handshake. Persistence was the key.

"You're so quiet back there," said Mother. "Are you daydreaming?"

"What else is there to do?" I said.

Jesus, I was getting so snarky. The woman was just trying to be conversational.

Daddy's smiling reflection looked back at me in the rearview mirror.

"When Kennedy runs for a second term, you can vote for him," he said.

He loved going to these functions. The democratic process was Daddy's religion. I'd seen the scratch of his pen across dozens of checks at fundraisers. A mitzvah, or payback, for the gift of our beautiful life, he said. Immigrant gratitude builds a great nation, Daddy said.

"Imagine what this country would be like with Nixon as president?" Mother said.

They both laughed.

"All Nixon had to do to get elected to Congress was lie," I said. "If he keeps lying, he could be president."

"Don't be ridiculous," said Mother.

There was silence, except for the dry desert wind whipping past the windows.

Daddy pulled into the parking lot as the sun set over Maison Jaussaud's. On the roof of the restaurant was a giant neon-green cactus. The pink adobe building had the only civilized dining on the outskirts of town. Beyond that, there were plowed fields that spread toward the Tehachapi mountains, the ridge route, and the pee-colored skies of Los Angeles.

Daddy parked our white Cadillac in the row of Cadillacs. It looked like all the wallets were inside. No sleek rental limo, so I guess Kennedy hadn't made it from the airport yet.

We climbed out of the cool leather seats into the baking heat. I felt sweat start to wet my silk pits. We pushed through wide wooden doors into a cloud scented with butter, wine, and garlic. Mother was always pink-faced with pleasure at Jaussaud's.

Jacques, the owner, greeted us with a big smile and a little bow. In Bakersfield you didn't kiss men on both cheeks like in France, or worse, give their wives a peck.

"*Bonsoir,* doctor," Jacques said in his musical accent. "*Bonsoir,* Madame and Mademoiselle. Your party is in the Fleur-de-Lis Room tonight."

He winked at me. "*Ça va?*" he said, encouraging my high school French. "*Aimez-vous John Kennedy?*"

"*Mais non, Monsieur Jacques,*" I said. "*J'aime Teddy!*"

He laughed. He thought I was funny from that time I made Mother drive me out to his restaurant with my shoebox full of live snails from our lawn. I'd read that the French eat snails. I thought I could make a lot of money since we had an infestation in the backyard. But Jacques said that to make them into edible escargots, I would have to feed them truffles and a fine Château Margaux.

"*Bon appetite*," Jacques said, walking us past Le Bar Louis Quatorze and delivering us personally to the Fleur-de-Lis Room.

"*Merci, Jacques*," said Mother.

The room was packed with all the Democrats in Bakersfield. They were dancing, chatting, and, of course, drinking. Dems were a minority in redneck central, but at least we could fill one large room.

French Impressionists prints hung on the knotty pine walls in gilded frames. We sat under one of Monet's paintings of water lilies. Our white tablecloth was starched and ironed. Pretty chichi for Bakersfield. Mother took off her gloves, elegant and slow—one finger at a time, like they do in the movies. She put them by her monogrammed plate.

Jimmy's Ballroom Band, dressed in white tuxes, played "Pennies from Heaven." Mother hummed along with the band and whispered, "'Pennies from Heaven' is an odd selection for a fundraiser." Responding to her humor, Daddy did his usual shoulder-shaking silent laughter that always ended in a slight cough.

I looked past all the party faces and tried to spot the door where Kennedy might enter. How could I grab him and get Teddy's phone number? I was jittery in the way I liked to be jittery. My knee was bouncing.

Mother leaned over and whispered, "Stop it."

Joseph W. Tucker, a tax attorney, sidled up to our table with his new wife and four kids from his previous wife. He was famous for accidentally setting his former wife's hair on fire at a barbecue last summer.

"Hi, Doc," he said. "Your daughter's a knockout." He didn't mean it.

"Thank you, Joe." Daddy smiled. He knew what was coming.

"Doc, I got this thing in my wrist. I think it's a bone spur . . . "

Daddy couldn't go anywhere without the conversation turning orthopedic.

"Love to see you at the office, Joe. Right now, I promised my favorite girl a dance."

Daddy grabbed my hand and swung me out on the dance floor. I twirled in an easy arc, his guiding hand on my back as we moved. Never a misstep in Daddy's arms.

"When is John Kennedy coming?" I said as we danced past the orchestra.

"He'll speak after we've eaten," said Daddy. "I'm so glad you're interested."

I couldn't tell him the only thing that interested me was getting my hands on Monsieur Teddy.

As the song ended, Daddy swept us back to Mother with an artful two, three, and dip.

"Daddy, you're a classy dancer," I said.

He squeezed my hand softly.

"It's nice to have my daughter's approval," he said.

Didn't Daddy know I approved of him? Did I never say it? I'd have to remember that parents could use a pat on the back too.

The band struck up, "Just a Lucky So-and-So."

Daddy and Mother danced off together. None of the other couples were as smooth as my parents. After the dance, Mother sat down, dabbing at her glow.

"Hon, sit up, please," whispered Mother. "Is that gum?"

I stuck the wad under the plate.

Hors d'oeuvres arrived and after that our coq au vin. Since we didn't drink, Mother ordered cokes. They were always served with tiny colorful umbrellas. *Parapluie* in French. I twirled mine and got a little coke on the tablecloth.

When dinner was over, potbellied Judge Brigg, lurched onto the stage in a brown suit, white shirt, and yellow tie that made him look like a buttered potato. His speech was too long and clichéd. We'd heard it all before. One goofus introduced another goofus in the Democratic party lineup, each promising to keep it short. I kicked off my high heels under the table. Not that I didn't understand ambition. I just didn't want to listen to it.

"Where's Kennedy?" I whispered to Mother.

"Exactly," whispered Mother, stifling a yawn behind her napkin.

Finally Judge Brigg returned to the podium. "And now, ladies and gentlemen, the next president of the United States. Please welcome Senator John Fitzgerald Kennedy!"

Mother and I sat up, fully awake. I wriggled back into my shoes. We gave a standing ovation as Kennedy walked in from the side door. He strode up on the small stage, adjusted the microphone, and paused as everyone sat down.

Everyone but me. I kept standing, smiling so he'd notice me. He looked right at me. I gave him a little wave.

Mother tugged at my dress.

"What are you doing?" she whispered.

I sat slowly, trying to catch his eye again.

"Thank you for that introduction, Judge Brigg," said Senator Kennedy. "Good evening, ladies and gentlemen. I am John Fitzgerald Kennedy, and I want to be your president."

There were cheers and applause that seemed endless.

His Boston accent sounded like he was imitating Teddy in a higher octave. His body was nothing like Teddy's. There was something pale and disappointing about him. His shoulders hunched uncomfortably over a shallow chest. He kept stroking his tie with the flat of his hand.

"I hope you realize the responsibility I carry," said Kennedy. "I'm the only person standing between Richard Nixon and the White House."

More endless cheers and applause.

Senator Kennedy continued his speech in a hesitating manner, almost as if he hadn't memorized it. But his words were thoughtful. Then, as he warmed up, he said, "Together let us explore the stars and conquer the deserts, eradicate disease, tap the ocean depths, and encourage the arts and commerce. If art is to nourish the roots of our culture, then society must set the artist free to follow his vision wherever it takes him."

This was the first political speech I'd heard that talked about art. It was poetic, but down to earth. Kennedy went on to paint his vision for the country's future. I strained to hear his every word over the air conditioning.

"Friends, let us not seek a Republican answer or a Democratic answer, but the *right* answer."

That was the America Daddy had talked about. A country that was everyone's responsibility.

Kennedy ended with a promise. He said we could count on him to lead us out of the divisive McCarthy era into a world with humanity and equality for all.

I'd never felt inspired like this by a politician's words. Not even with Teddy. I clapped until my hands hurt. The crowd of Dems cheered him like crazy. Maybe this guy really did have a chance to be president!

Daddy put his arms around me and Mother. He was as happy as I'd ever seen him.

Kennedy gave us the Kennedy smile. He looked so much like Teddy at that moment, I almost plotzed.

Then Judge Brigg followed his red-veined nose back to the microphone.

"Senator," he said, "you are one hell of a speaker. Pardon my French, ladies. I'm going to close this part of our Democratic national fundraiser because our future president has to catch a plane to Fresno. Thank you for coming to Bakersfield, Senator."

He rapped the podium for attention. "All right, folks," said the judge. "You can have John Fitzgerald Kennedy in the White House or Richard M. Nixon. Your choice. Dig deep."

Kennedy waved and smiled as he headed for the exit.

Hey, wait a minute. Come back!

Kennedy was being rushed through the door by a big bald man and a dark-haired woman who was looking at her watch. Crap! I shoved back my chair. I could still catch him.

Mother grabbed my arm. "Where are you going?"

"I gotta talk to him!" I said

"Are you nuts?" she said. "You stay right here and wait for us."

I pulled my arm out of her grip. "It's important!"

Daddy was writing a check. "Hold on, hon," he said.

"Hurry up Daddy." I jiggled in place.

"Stop it," whispered Mother. "What's wrong with you?"

All over the Fleur-de-Lis Room ballpoint pens glided over light-blue checks. A small fortune dropped into baskets passed around by leggy cheerleaders dressed in the short blue-and-white uniforms of Bakersfield High, with oil well logos on their chests and our motto: *Once a Driller, Always a Driller.*

Daddy dropped his check in the basket. I grabbed his arm and hauled him out of the ballroom. I ran on ahead, pushing through the entrance door. What were the chances Kennedy would still be in the parking lot?

The Bakersfield night had cooled down. Jaussaud's giant neon cactus lit the cars a pale green. And there, on the other side of the parking lot, was Kennedy. He was still here!

The black limo had its hood up. A shirt-sleeved chauffeur was bent over the motor. Kennedy looked at his watch. The woman and the bald man seemed pretty upset. I knew a heaven-sent opportunity when I saw it.

"Need a ride to the airport?" I shouted and ran across the parking lot toward them.

Mother and Daddy had no choice but to follow.

Daddy caught up to me, breathing hard. "Can we help you?"

Thank you, Daddy! Kennedy and his staff of two picked up their briefcases.

"Looks like we could use some help, if it's not inconvenient," said Kennedy.

He was about a foot taller than me, and his skin looked old in the pale green cactus light. His eyes were circled dark. I got into step next to him as we walked toward our car.

"Your speech was great," I said. "I liked the Peace Corps idea."

"I encourage you to apply," said Kennedy. "We need good young people like yourself."

"I really liked Teddy's speech last month."

"All the girls like Teddy," Kennedy said with a little smile. His lips looked chapped.

"I'm sure the girls liked your speech, too," I said.

I didn't want him to feel left out just because he didn't have any sex appeal.

A few more yards to the car and then I'd have the privacy I needed to show him my autograph book. He'd see Teddy had written that he wanted my help. All I needed was Teddy's phone number.

"Senator!" yelled Judge Brigg. The judge hurried toward us. His tie was flying. His gut was bouncing. He puffed up to us with his wife in tow.

"I just heard about the limo," he said. "Hop in. I'll drive you."

The judge pointed to his car. It had some dings in the fenders. He didn't look like he was in the greatest shape to drive anyone. It was a clear case of dibs. I was ready to leap on the judge and fight him for Kennedy.

"Hey, we offered first," I said.

"Sorry," said Mother. "A little case of hero worship has got her excited."

She took out her Minox camera.

"Senator!" said Mother. "A quick picture before you leave. It'll mean so much to her."

Hey, blame it on me. Mother gave me a little shove and I stood next to Kennedy.

The black-haired woman pointed to her watch. Kennedy nodded at her and turned to me.

"It sounds like you're interested in the campaign," he said. "I know Teddy and I would both appreciate your help here, locally."

"Really?" I said. "What do I do?"

"Say cheese," said Mother, fumbling with the camera and snapping a shot.

"Ma'am, I'm sorry." The dark-haired woman was climbing into the back seat of the judge's convertible. "We're very late. Senator, please. We have to go."

Kennedy pulled a card out of his pocket and handed it to me. "It's our headquarters. They'll put you in touch with someone."

"Thanks!" I gave him my biggest smile. I wished I had his teeth.

"Write and let us know how the campaign's going here," said Kennedy.

He climbed in the back seat of the judge's convertible.

"I will!" I said. I was family now!

Judge Brigg's car roared out of the parking lot with his pale wife beside him clutching the door handle. Kennedy's head looked small in the back seat, sandwiched between his two helpers.

The convertible swung out onto the highway and sped away into the night. I realized I'd forgotten to ask him to sign my autograph book.

Daddy put his arms around me and Mother. His voice was soft with emotion. "I've never felt so hopeful as I am now, with the possibility of this man as president," he said.

I tucked Kennedy's card in my autograph book. I wondered if tonight was too soon to write.

CHAPTER 18
THE FALL OF MISTER SNOW

Know thy enemy!
—Mother

Bakersfield, 1961

I was always slightly mesmerized watching Mr. Snow.

He paced slowly in front of the classroom in a nicely fitted blazer with pleated dark pants and an East Coast reserve. His dark burr haircut stood up over a high intellectual forehead. With brilliant black eyes, the man saw deeply into our distracted teen souls, insisting, against all evidence to the contrary, that we were worthy.

"Ladies and gentlemen," he said. He never called us boys and girls. "Of all the poets we read last week, who am I quoting here? *No man is an island, entire of itself; every man is a piece of the continent . . .*"

I shot my hand up directly in his line of vision. He nodded at me. His dark eyes looked just about as excited as I felt.

"John Donne?" I said.

"Are you asking a question or giving me an answer?" he said with a smile.

Oh, I forgot. We were supposed to answer like we knew what we were talking about.

"John Donne," I said, louder.

Mr. Snow ignored the class snickering. He nodded to Billy Raine, the constant doodler.

"Mr. Raine," he said, "do you agree with Donne's assessment of the human condition? Are our hearts attached to the mainland of humanity? Are we peninsulas or are we merely solitary islands?"

Billy raised the pen off his sketch, a little gruff at the interruption.

"We're islands!" he said. "We're born alone, jerked around, and die alone. Then we go to some kind of heavenly peace. Which you friggin' never get at home!"

He got a few grunts of approval with that line.

"Now, class, if we're all truly alone in life," said Mr. Snow, "as Mr. Raine so colorfully expressed, is love then only a fleeting solace? An illusion? A sucker punch?"

Hands shot in the air. Mr. Snow's Socratic routine kept us digging. We all had to have an opinion. That was part of the grade. He beamed at our heated discussion.

The hour with Snow passed so quickly. I was always breathless by the end. Who knew my brain could feel so good? I kept wondering how this super teacher ended up in Bakersfield, which, according to Mother, was the farthest point from intellectual stimulation in the universe.

His subject was world literature. And he used it to lead us out of the insular village of our minds, and into a world we didn't know existed. He gave us a structure and a way of questioning that led us to answers. Those answers gave us confidence. Mr. Snow's lofty goal was for each of us to discover ourselves, so we could construct a meaningful life in relationship to our society. The philosophies of these brilliant authors was a nudge to get us there.

"What do Tolstoy's characters tell us about his belief system?" he asked.

I just hoped the front office wasn't paying too much attention to

Snow's curriculum because Tolstoy was a big *macher* in the Commie world. How could Snow not know that every Russian, living or dead, was considered a Cold War threat in Bakersfield? If Daddy's secret, that he was born in Russia, ever got out, he'd never get a single solitary patient.

One day I got to class early. Snow asked me what I thought of a print he'd just hung up. It was a bearded man, but he was painted in pieces and looked like a broken mirror.

"The painting is called 'The Rabbi,'" said Mr. Snow. "It's by Marc Chagall in his Cubist period. Chagall was a famous Jewish Russian painter."

My heart stopped. "How did you know I'm a Russian Jew?"

He looked surprised. "I didn't," he said.

"Well, don't tell anyone," I said.

"You have my word," he said.

I felt a little stupid. And what was a Cubist period anyway? It sounded like math.

After class I biked to the downtown library and looked it up. The next day I told Mr. Snow that I didn't like Cubism. Why paint people in pieces when it was hard enough to paint them whole?

"You can't imagine how delighted I am to hear you say that," he said. "Take my book on Cubism home. Spend some time really looking at the pictures and then write three more reasons why you hate Cubism."

Tearing apart a whole art movement was delicious fun. Especially now that I knew what it was.

That year with Snow was all about growth that had nothing to do with hormones. It almost made me regret graduating. At home, I couldn't stop talking about him.

"Enough, already," said Mother. "If you mention that man's name again . . ."

Between classes, Mary Ellen told me she was on the school paper now and she planned to investigate Snow.

"I sense an exposé," she said. "We don't know a damned thing about him. He could be a Commie. My Dad said they recruit kids."

"First, your Dad's a moron," I said. "And second, even bullshit talk like that can hurt a guy in this town."

Mary Ellen shrugged. "I'm doing a Dick Tracy on him anyway, so there," she said.

One cool thing Mary Ellen found out about Snow was, he had a rich dad in Detroit in the auto industry. Which would explain why Snow had a four-speed honkin' red-and-white Pontiac convertible with a V-8 engine and leather interior. This prim little man in such a muscle car. It just didn't fit our image of him.

There wasn't much more she could find out about him, so he remained a man of mystery. Who doesn't fall in love with a mystery? Even Mary Ellen was smitten. Besides, he was by far the best teacher we ever had. The two of us decided to let Snow know how much we appreciated him, and wrote him a funny poem using all the authors' names we'd studied. I copied the poem on nice art paper and we went to his classroom after school to deliver the poem. He usually lingered over student reports. He never seemed anxious to get away from us, unlike most teachers who raced out after the last bell.

But this time, he was sitting at his desk with the principal towering over him.

"You need to adjust your thinking," said the principal. "I suggest you consider this."

He handed Snow a sheet of paper and strode past us down the hall like he was pissed.

You didn't have to be a scholar to read Snow's face. His sallow skin had turned a chalky white. His hands looked like they might be shaking as he crumpled the paper the principal had given him. He threw it in the trash can. When he saw us, he grabbed his briefcase and headed for the door.

"Good afternoon, ladies," he said. "If you'll excuse me."

He walked down the hall just as fast as he could go. Mary Ellen had more of a pulp-mystery mind than I did. She scurried over and pulled the crumpled paper out of the trash can and spread it on his clean desk.

It was an invitation to the faculty of Bakersfield High and their families for a catered smorgasbord dinner in a couple of weeks. It promised a lecture about "A New America." The address of the party was on an exclusive street, Golf Course Drive. The offer came from a group called the John Birch Society.

"Research," said Mary Ellen.

We left our poem on his desk and spent the afternoon at the library.

The John Birch Society had been founded in 1958 by a rich candy maker named Welch in Massachusetts. *With God's help, a better world* was Welch's motto. The John Birch Society was anti-Semitic, anti-Mormon, anti-Masonic, anti-Black, anti-Latin, anti-Asian, anti-homosexual, and anti-everyone who wasn't a white Christian. Welch declared that the civil rights movement and fluoride were Communist plots, and that President Dwight D. Eisenhower was a Communist dupe.

The Birchers had found a home in Bakersfield. No surprise there.

Snow obviously wasn't going to the Fascist pig-out, so Mary Ellen, Rolly, and I decided to go, and find out what was what with these jerks. Maybe we could help Snow.

As Mother always said, "Know thy enemy."

Mary Ellen held up the wrinkled paper.

"I'll iron it," she said, and grinned. "This could be a big scoop!"

We inched along at five miles an hour, windshield wipers going full-bore. I'd lost the coin toss, so I sat like a fool on the hood of Rolly's dad's Pontiac, squinting for asphalt. Tule fog had rolled in quick, like it did, and took us by surprise. These sudden big bales of white vapor caused fender benders all over town.

My ass was warm but the rest of me was shivering. I couldn't see more than a few feet ahead. Our beams were slowly shifting over the center white line. A nearly invisible truck was coming toward us.

I banged twice on the hood: *two for right.*

Rolly veered just in time to avoid a collision. I hung onto the hood. The truck passed slowly stirring heavy mist over my oxfords. Rolly and Mary Ellen were dry and warm in the front seat, with the ironed invitation in her purse.

"How we doing?" Rolly teased out his window.

"Screw you!" I shouted back.

I stared into the heavy mist for any sign of Golf Club Drive. I bolstered myself with Mother's words at dinner.

"I'm glad you're educating yourself about this John Bircher insanity. Just don't tell them you're Jewish."

I'd reassured her. "No one shoots kids at a smorgasbord."

A small street sign was barely visible on the right-hand side of the road. I wiped the mist off my eyelashes. Golf Club Drive.

"There it is!" I pounded twice on the hood.

Rolly swerved right and took the turn a little too fast. When he stopped suddenly, I nearly shot off the hood.

"Come on, get in," yelled Rolly.

I climbed into the backseat and pulled his sports blanket around my shoulders. The road was smooth with a barbed-wire fence on either side of the lane. Up ahead was a white blur that turned into outdoor lights that lit up a misty Southern-style mansion with huge columns.

Rolly drove us into the circular driveway, gravel snapping like popcorn under the car's wet treads. Ghostly outlines of trees were bent over Cadillacs parked in the turnaround. The three of us climbed out of the Pontiac, ready to fake our way into whatever they had going on.

A fat man waddled toward us out of the mist. He was about four feet tall and four feet wide. The little fellow would probably look the same any which way you turned him. Fog made his big eyes look like they were running down his cheeks.

"Howdy, folks. I'm Arliss Busker," he said. "I'll need to see your invite."

Mary Ellen handed it over. It had gotten crumply again in her purse. Arliss switched on a flashlight and made a show of unfolding, examining, nodding, and handing it back. He took a Dixie cup out of his pocket and spit dark tobacco chaw into it. It sounded so juicy my dinner steak curdled.

"You shouldn't-a showed up late," he said. "Mr. Jesse Bob don't like that."

"Sorry, Mr. Busker," said Rolly, zipping up his jacket. "But we passed an accident. I had to get out and tourniquet a woman."

Good one, Rolly!

"Much blood?" said Arliss Busker.

"Died in my arms," said Rolly with a sniff.

Mary Ellen put her hand over her mouth to keep the laugh in.

Arliss took a squinty bead on Rolly.

"Aw-right, y'all," he said.

We followed him to the side of the house. He unlocked a metal door. It swung open like a safe. Jesus, I was shivering again. We trooped down some metal steps and into a basement with a cement corridor lit with bright bulbs in metal cages. There were doors on either side. I had such an urge to shove one open. I guess this was one of those bomb shelters folks were building all over the country against the A-bomb. But this one was huge.

Arliss looked back at us.

"No Commies ever gonna git in this here bomb shelter," said Arliss.

He smiled proudly. His teeth were brown. What would happen to that stained smile if he knew our Trojan-horse asses were up to an exposé? At the end of the corridor, Arliss pushed through a wide door.

Inside, black-and-white checkered linoleum covered the huge basement floor. Most folks were gathered at the long smorgasbord table. At least people were dressed casually, so we didn't stick out. The principal was over at the bar, talking to a few faculty. Some kids were having fun at a Ping-Pong table. The showy chandelier reflected off the jukebox's plastic curves. Forty-fives stacked up. Buck Owens, Bakersfield's local boy, sang "Foolin' Around."

The three of us headed for the plattered eats—baked beans, barbecued ribs, hot greens, yellow grits, potato salad with raisins, coleslaw, red marshmallow Jell-O, and plenty of desserts. Rolly and Mary Ellen dove in. I'd eaten dinner, but no way I'd pass up that flakey, sugary hot apple pie. Christians sure knew how to bake.

I walked around slowly scarfing the treat and looking at what passed for art. A string of iron horseshoes were nailed to the wall in a pattern that looked like a giant rusted necklace. Cowboy lariats were starched and hung in the shape of horse heads. That showed some imagination. Guns racks were filled with shotguns, short guns, long guns, pistols, and rifles with scopes. There were framed paper targets of silhouetted human beings with several bullet holes in their hearts. They were signed, like art projects.

Arliss Busker got everyone's attention and herded us to the fold-out chairs lined up in front of a big wood podium. He seated the three of us in the front row. It was like a school assembly. Hopefully not as boring, because now we were kind of stuck here until the end.

After a few minutes, the same door we'd entered swung wide. A big man strode up to the podium. His gut hung over his silver belt buckle like a giant ripe pear. I knew Mr. Jesse Bob Williams from his pictures in the paper.

The legend of Jesse Bob Williams was short. During the Dust Bowl days, his family left a dirt-poor farm in Oklahoma and ended up on a dirt-poor farm in Bakersfield. Then, he and his father struck enough oil to light up Texas. He'd taken a degree in divinity at a Christian college, was president of the John Birch Society, and made sure everyone who wasn't white had a rough time.

Mother once said, "Mr. Jesse Bob's bankroll makes things grow that should be stillborn."

Mr. Jesse Bob swung up behind the podium, looking confident. His teeth were movie-star white. He looked down at us with shiny brown button eyes pushed into a clay-red face. He gave us a moment to admire his tan tailored cowboy suit with dark detailing and a leather lanyard held with a huge turquoise clip. His large hands grasped the wood podium on either side. He looked strong enough to lift it.

"Howdy, neighbors and friends!" he said. "Welcome! Welcome to y'all! Hope yer enjoying the food and drink. You can call me Jesse Bob here. Anywhere else, it's Mr. Williams to y'all."

He paused for a laugh, which he got. I felt the tug of his smile. His charisma melted all over us like grease.

"I'm the one providing this shindig on behalf of the John Birch Society. I am president and founding member of the Bakersfield chapter. Welcome to our first national gathering. Hallelujah."

Mary Ellen nudged me. *National.* We were in for some skinny.

"Let's get started, folks," said Mr. Jesse Bob.

He put his hand on his heart and turned to the American flag next to the podium.

We stood and put our hands over our hearts. A record of Kate Smith blasted "God Bless America." It was too loud. Mary Ellen rolled her eyes, but I got weirdly emotional. Kate Smith's high notes, the giant American flag, a strong smell of barbecue, my stomach full of hot apple pie. It's creepy how patriotic sentiment can sneak up on you.

We sat down and watched Mr. Jesse Bob light his cigar and puff it ruby red. He took it out of his mouth and curled those sun-hardened wrinkles into a deep frown of concern.

"My friends, thank you for coming. Some from far, some from close by. I love you all, so I'm gonna tell you the absolute truth, because the government won't! My friends, look over here at this map. Whataya see?"

Arliss and two men unveiled a big map of the world. It looked like a radish festival. Every country was some shade of red. Russia was the brightest. America was dark pink, with big stretches of deep crimson on either coast.

"It's pretty obvious that the Commies are taking over the world," said Mr. Jesse Bob. "Friends, if you want to keep the good life you got, you need to get your horses outta the burning barn and ride down those devils that's coming to get you. Ya'll know who I'm talking about. Let me hear you say it!"

"Commies!" shouted the crowd, raising their fists like Nazis in the newsreels.

My arm stayed down, my mouth stayed shut, but my mind was having the heaves. Holy crap. This was worse than I thought. The crowd's fear and anger were stirred. Mr. Jesse Bob slapped the podium.

"America is the last stronghold against Communism. That's the truth! THEY are everywhere. THEY are in government, in Hollywood, in the banks, in the schools. THEY are the Jews, the liberals, the Mormons, the homosexuals. The mongrel browns, yellows, and blacks with their civil rights all wrong. They are called Democrats! Who do we hate?"

"DEMOCRATS!" yelled the crowd.

Oh, my God! I shook inside. He was so dead-sure of those lies. If I were as ignorant as the other people in this room, I might be convinced by his fearsome lack of logic.

Mr. Jesse Bob pointed right at me, Mary Ellen, and Rolly.

"You. You young folks. You are the future! It's your responsibility to fight Communism back from the God-given shores of America! You're in good company for the battle. We got a special guest speaker tonight. Here's a real treat for y'all. Our junior college football quarterback. Dean David, come on out here, boy."

Dean David! Dean David! Who didn't have a crush on Dean David?

The crowd roared. Dean walked out blushing from behind the draped flag. His blond hair shone like sun on wheat. Football shoulders, slim waist, and a sweet angular face. He wore a white shirt and thin brown tie under his varsity jacket. His tight white Levi's got my attention.

Mr. Jesse Bob slapped Dean's shoulder. It sounded so solid.

"Like the song says," Mr. Jesse Bob said, "you're every guy's hero and every gal's dream."

Mr. Jesse Bob turned a little and winked at me and Mary Ellen. Yuk.

"Dean here is gonna share something deeply personal with y'all," he said.

Dean David looked like the last thing he wanted to do was share something personal. But to his credit, his Adam's apple bucked softly, and he swallowed his reluctance.

"I was asked to talk about my Christian beliefs. I don't usually share this with anyone, but Mr. Williams convinced me. You all are important, especially the younger folks here, in our fight against godless Communism."

He bowed his head like he was about to pray. Each sentence seemed hard for him. He raised his head, looking as vulnerable as a wounded duck.

"I was a sinner," said Dean David. "God punished me with abundance, which I gave to all those sinning women. Over and over and over . . ."

"Move it along, Dean," said Mr. Jesse Bob.

"Yessir. Well, one night in the presence of a sinning woman, I felt the pain of Jesus in my heart. I couldn't move. I cried out, 'Help me, Lord.' I felt his hand touch me. And the pain was gone. I felt cleansed in my mind and body." Dean sobbed happily. "I've been celibate ever since! Thank you, Jesus!"

His neon-blue eyes flickered at Mary Ellen.

"Hallelujah!" yelled the crowd.

"Like Mr. Jesse Bob said, those godless Commies got to be tackled and brought down!" said Dean.

Everyone shouted. "Tackle 'em! Bring 'em down! Lock 'em up!"

Mr. Jesse Bob waited a bit, and then motioned for everyone to quiet down.

"Thank you, Dean David," said Mr. Jesse Bob. "You are God's warrior You see, kids, it was Dean David's belief in Jesus that made him the man he is today. A warrior. Y'all are warriors too. When your heart is with Jesus, you will recognize the enemies of decency, for they come in many forms. Not just Communists and Democrats. You will know those others by their abominations, by their unholy devotion to sins of the mind and body. Their evil teachings destroy our children, our American way of life! Who am I talking about? You know them, for they dare to walk among us. Who are they?"

The crowd wanted to shout something, but they seemed as confused as I was about who "they" were?

"PERVERTS!" shouted Jesse Bob.

There was a stunned pause. And then. "YES!" shouted the crowd. "PERVERTS!"

"My friends, beware of their disguises." Mr. Jesse Bob's voice grew soft, deep, concerned. "Some are teachers. They suck the young into their filth. You, leaders of our schools. Beware the rot within!"

There was nothing subtle about that. Mary Ellen glanced at me. Her eyes said, *Oh shit*. I looked over at the principal. He was nodding. Teachers? He meant Snow. These Bible thumpers wanted to string him up for teaching Tolstoy? *That's* what they call perversion?

"You kids in the front row, come on up here," said Mr. Jesse Bob.

I shrunk in my seat. But Arliss Busker herded the three of us up to the podium.

"You kids," said Mr. Jesse Bob. "Tell the audience why you came out here tonight. Y'all came as God fearin' Christian seekers, didn't you?"

I saw the principal in the audience smiling at me.

"We came for information," said Rolly.

"Hear that, folks?" He turned to the crowd. "These are smart kids. That's who we're here for! The smart kids!"

"Sir, as a future leader of America," said Rolly, "I'd like to know more about the Bircher's plan for our school."

Mr. Jesse Bob smiled. "We're all worried about our educational system, son. The John Birch Society will get those perverted liberal teachers so fired they ain't never gonna teach again."

"What teachers do you mean?" said Rolly.

Oh, God, Rolly. Leave it alone!

Mr. Jesse Bob snorted. "The kind we don't want in our schools or anywhere near our children. You see them every day and I think y'all know in your heart who they are."

I wanted to pick up the podium and bring it down on Mr. Jesse Bob's head.

"Excuse me, Mr. Jesse Bob," I said, my voice quaking all over the place. "I hope you don't mean Mr. Snow. He's the best teacher we ever had. There's nothing perverted about teaching world literature. Couldn't you just ask him to stop teaching Russian authors rather than get him fired?"

Mr. Jesse Bob busted out laughing. He backed off from the podium and kept on laughing and slapping his knee until he had a coughing fit.

What the hell? I didn't say anything funny.

"Young lady," said Mr. Jesse Bob. "I won't say straight out what that man is in polite company. If you don't know, I ain't gonna be the one to break the bad news. But it's strapping boys like this we wanna keep away from his kind."

Mr. Jesse Bob put his hand on Rolly's shoulder. Rolly pulled himself free.

"That man is worth ten of you!" said Rolly.

Oh, my God, Rolly! I edged back from the podium.

Mary Ellen backed away too. Would they let us out of here?

Mr. Jesse Bob got the strangest smile on his red face. He turned to the audience.

"Folks, seems like we been invaded by dupes. These fresh-faced little souls believe the lies of their teacher, a man of unmentionable abominations. You see how easy it is to be fooled. It's not their fault. Their brains have been poisoned. Young man, y'all are defending a foulness that you can't begin to understand. Boys, better escort these kids out."

Mr. Jesse Bob dismissed us with a wave of his big hand. The principal and the audience frowned at us as we were led out the door.

Arliss Busker and his goon squad made sure we were in the car and driving down Golf Club Drive before they turned back to the house. The tule fog had sunk low to the ground so it was easier to see our way to the main road.

We drove along, the three of us in the wide front seat, silent as the fog.

"Rolly, that was really stupid," I said. "And brave."

"Fucking asshole!" said Rolly. "If he knew I was as gay as Snow, he'd probably have shot me."

"Snow's not gay," I said.

Mary Ellen roared, looking at me like I was crazy. "Lord love a redneck! How *do* you stay so dense?"

"He *is*?" I said. My heart almost stopped. I was so in love with that man.

"How do you think he ended up in a dead-end dump like Bakersfield?" said Rolly. "You think this is something new for him?"

We drove in silence for a while. My world had shifted.

"Just drive by his apartment," I said.

We knew where he lived. We'd driven past his place a million times just for fun, daring each other to knock on his door. We never did.

A heavy mist hid most of his building. Snow's fancy car was parked by the curb and the trunk was open.

Rolly parked across the street from the car. We sat and waited to see what was going on.

Mr. Snow came down the sidewalk, lugging a huge suitcase. He wore a dark sweater and denims. This was the first time I'd seen him without a suit on.

It was clear that he was leaving. But how could he just walk out? We had a month of school left.

Another man, blond and younger, helped him stuff the suitcase into the trunk. Mr. Snow slammed it shut. It sounded so final. They stood for a moment looking at each other. The way the two of them stood together, I guess I saw what I needed to see.

As we got out of the Pontiac and crossed the street, Mr. Snow saw us. He put his hands on his hips and eyed the ground in front of him. When we got close, he looked up.

"How did you know?" he said.

"We didn't," I said.

"Just in the neighborhood," said Mary Ellen.

"We went to that Bircher thing. Thought maybe we could help you," said Rolly.

"You did?" Snow looked exhausted. "Thank you."

He nodded at the beautiful blond man. "My nephew, Frank," said Mr. Snow.

Frank was leaning against the car, ignoring us.

"I'm grateful you stopped by," said Mr. Snow. "At least I get to say good-bye to you three."

"We didn't know it was going to be good-bye," I said.

Mr. Snow smiled at us. "You'll be fine. There'll be a sub, but I've put in your grades. You'd get triple A+, if there were such a thing. I can't begin to tell you how proud I am of you and the progress you've made. It's been an honor to be your teacher. And thank you for your beautiful poem. I have it in my suitcase."

I didn't know if I could keep from crying.

He shook each of our hands as if we were a squad that had taken a dangerous hill. If I was braver, I'd have pulled him in for a hug. Just to feel the whole of him once.

"You'll do great things," he said. "It's not an easy world, but it'll help to remember that last poem we read. Do you remember the last lines?"

Fly, young winged soldier, in battles of the night. Love, thy love of self, will be thy greatest fight.

He tossed the keys to Frank. "You drive," he said, and trembled a sigh.

Frank put his arm around Mr. Snow's thin shoulders and gave him a hug.

They got in. Frank gunned the motor and spewed exhaust all over us.

They shot off down the street. Mr. Snow waved without turning around.

I shouted after him. "I still hate Cubism!"

I knew that would make him happy.

CHAPTER 19
PROM NIGHT

Someday you'll thank me.
—Mother

Bakersfield, May 1961

"See you for a run when I get back from hang-gliding," said Willard.

That was how our last conversation ended.

Willard's father let him go up in a glider and a rough wind brought him down. The glider broke apart and so did Willard. My running buddy was gone, the boy who was going to take me into space with him when he was a man.

I went to the funeral. Mary Ellen and Rolly were there to hold my hand. I had my tears under control. Crying just wets stuff over and feels awful. Looking at his coffin, I tried to make his broken body unreal inside that box.

Mostly, I'd go home after school and sleep. I dreamt that Willard got over being dead and we went to the prom. I could just see him in a light-blue tux. Not that he'd asked me yet. But we both knew we'd be together on the big wingding night. Maybe someday, when I was dead too, we'd be in touch again. We'd scuff things up on a golden dance floor with other dead couples. All those songs we'd remember. "Rock Around the Clock." That was ours.

Keeping that stupid dream in my head kept me going.

Then Mother said, even without Willard, I had to go to the prom.

"You don't want to look back in twenty years," said Mother, "and be sorry you missed your prom. Someday you'll thank me. It's too bad about Willard. But grief should be brief."

Grief should be brief? Jesus! And when would that *someday* be? When would I feel like thanking Mother for making me do the million things I didn't want to do?

A week after Willard's funeral, Mother railroaded on ahead with prom plans and set me up with her bridge friend's son, Hiram. Who names their kid Hiram?

Mother picked the prom dress. Red and shiny. The fit might've shown cleavage if I'd had any. I did have great legs. All in all, a good package if you weren't a tit man. What bothered me most about this prom dress thing was the waste of money. I was going to wear this gorgeous formal once. Just once on a hot sweaty Bakersfield night. And then what? Bag it for a daughter who would one day say, "But Mommy, it's so old-fashioned!"

And Willard, poor Willard. He would've showed up in a rented light-blue tux that smelled like moth balls, not giving a shit what I wore. He just wanted to hang out with me.

Goddamnit, Willard! Are you watching this?

On the night of the prom, the doorbell rang. It was Hiram. My first blind date. He stood there like he was in front of a firing squad. A stiff dud-head. Reed-tall, severe haircut, and smart, skittery eyes behind thick glasses. A debate-team darling.

He shackled my wrist with a gardenia corsage and led me to the car.

I was embarrassed to be seen with him. For one thing, you don't want to look too smart at Bakersfield High, and he did. Walking up to the wingding, I didn't let him hold my hand. Inside the cafeteria it was a swamp. Wilted crepe from condensed kid sweat. Music amped too loud. The band was totally off their beat. I heard that the drummer had broken his arm at the annual James Dean drag race.

A lot of the kids stood around drinking punch. Some danced. Others signed the cardboard mascot. A few nicer kids came up and said, "Sorry to hear about Willard."

"Thanks for reminding me," I said, and slumped into one of the foldout chairs. Hiram brought over two plastic cups of red punch. He set one in front of me. I saw red on his cuff. The doofus must have spilled. I kind of sneered at him.

"You should be nicer to me," said Hiram. He sat next to me and shouted over the band. "I spent three-fifty on your corsage."

I took the gardenia off my wrist and threw it at him.

"Get a refund," I said.

Jesus! I was taking it out on him because he wasn't Willard. I was such a shit!

"Hey, Harem," I said. "I'm sorry."

"Hiram," he shouted. "My name is *Hiram*."

I knew that. He was just a nice guy who'd make someone a nice husband, if that's all you wanted. He had no idea what to do with someone like me. I should have come to the prom alone, but no one does that.

"Why'd you want to come to the prom with me?" he shouted.

"I didn't want to come at all," I shouted. "My boyfriend got killed so my mother set this up."

"Oh. OK. That's rough. But I seem to annoy you," he shouted. "Maybe I should leave you alone?"

"Would you? Please?" I shouted back. "Catch me in an hour. You can take me home."

Hiram put his punch cup down, got up and walked away. What a relief.

But to his credit, he had responded to my pissiness like a reasonable grownup. Left me to rant alone. I really did just want to go home.

Hiram beelined to Marlee, a thin wallflower-type genius with glasses. Oh yeah, she was on the debate team too. They got smiley and danced. Never mind who her date was. She and Hiram fit together like the last two pieces of a puzzle. He'd probably marry her, and they'd have kids, and he'd work his way up in the new aerospace industry and die bald. Maybe they'd have true love. Something I figured would never find me. Willard being gone. That was a sure sign.

I watched Mary Ellen dancing with Rolly. They'd been such good friends to me during the funeral, but Rolly had the bigger heart. Right now, I could use a hug from him. His tan glowed and his black hair rested over his collar, a real dangerous look. He was getting ready to go out into the world and make his debut. *Broadway, here I come!* And Mary Ellen, with her dark hair, free and wavy. She was more than ready to leave her crazy family behind and waft onto the stage of any summer stock that would have her. There was something wild and full of neon promise about those two tonight.

Bored, I picked a blue crayon out of the box and drew on the butcher paper tablecloth. I didn't need anyone else. I sketched Darrel the quarterback with his team buddies chugging from a not very hidden pint. Lucky for them, the chaperones were flirting with each other. Darrel got caught at the last football game with vodka in his snow cone and was almost expelled.

Mary Ellen and Rolly came over and sat down next to me. Mary Ellen's curvy thighs spread under her green taffeta formal.

"Lemme see what you did," Mary Ellen shouted over the band noise.

I tore off my drawing and handed it to her. She was my biggest fan because I always made people look uglier than they were.

"Memories," she said, and stuffed the sketch in her purse. "Where's your date?"

I nodded at Hiram, dancing eyeglasses to eyeglasses with his future bride.

"Prince Boring," said Mary Ellen. She took off her heels and gave her toes a tug.

"The biggest launch party of our lives," said Rolly. "Look at us."

"Oh, fuck this shit," shouted Mary Ellen, "I can't hear a thing!"

She shoved her feet back in the heels and the three of us pushed through the double doors. A full moon lit up the quad. We sank onto the cement benches. Ah, that breeze sucked my sweaty skin dry. A couple was making out and scooted away. One woozy guy passed us a pint. I took a big slug and felt better.

"Where is it written," said Rolly, "that graduates can't celebrate their liberation at the site of their own choosing?"

"That's just what I was thinking, only not as elegantly stated," I said.

"Let's get the hell out of here!" said Mary Ellen.

We got up and straightened our fancy duds.

"I should say goodbye to Hiram," I said.

"Hiram's found the love of his creepy life," said Mary Ellen. "Let's boogie."

Ten minutes later we were driving along Chester Avenue crammed in the front seat of Rolly's dad's Pontiac. Rolly pulled out a pint from under his seat and we shared it to empty. No regrets tonight. We were flying high. Rolly gunned the motor at a red stoplight.

"Where do you guys want to go?" he said.

That question always brought out the best in me. "Venice," I said.

When they laughed, I said, "Venice Beach."

Mary Ellen got it right away and clapped me on the knee. "You're thinking the Beats?

"I'm thinking the Gas House!" I said.

"Beatnik central," said Rolly. "Cool."

We were such fans. I'd always wanted to take my bongos down among them.

"Ladies," said Rolly, "you're paying for the gas!"

We had a whole long evening ahead of us where we wouldn't be missed. This was our glory night! We were free! We were drunk! We were almost grown-ups!

"Fuck all!" shouted Rolly and tossed the empty pint out the window. It shattered against a metal mailbox. We looked around to see if any cops had noticed. Then we laughed. A nervous laugh. I mean, we weren't thugs.

The Pontiac roared us along US Highway 99 up the ridge route and through the dusty Tehachapis.

"Hey, Rolly," I said. "Do you know where Venice Beach is?"

"Hell, no," he said. "I just know the way out of town."

Mary Ellen laughed. "What's to know? You can't miss Los Angeles. The ocean is on the right."

I loved how loose these guys hung.

We sang with the windows wide open. "Three little maids from school are we, filled to the brim with girlish glee. Three little maids from school!" We sang all the Gilbert and Sullivan songs we knew and that got us as far as the City of Angels.

Rolly pulled over to a lit-up café. We all needed a cup of joe. Sitting at the counter, my head started clearing. I looked at the clock on the wall. It had taken us two hours to get to L.A. It was nine. And we weren't even at Venice Beach. Two hours or more back. Mother said to be home no later than one. That meant we had to leave Venice before eleven. Shit. That gave us forty-five minutes to find the Beats.

"Drink up, you guys," I said.

We asked the sad-faced waitress where Venice Beach was. She didn't know. She lived above the café with her husband and had never been very far down the road.

"Look at you kids," she said, shoving the sugar and cream at us. "My prom night was the best night of my life. Then I got married."

There was a truck driver sitting on one of the stools. He said his name was Burly and he offered to draw us a map to Venice Beach.

"You kids should stop at the Gas House," said the truck driver. "They got great cinnamon rolls."

"Bitchin'!" I said. "I didn't know they had food!"

Slowly, too slowly, Burly scrawled us a careful map on his coffee-stained napkin.

"Could you hurry a little?" I said.

The map should have got us there fast, but Rolly made a wrong turn somewhere. Finally, we found a sign: *To Venice Beach.* We turned south from Market to Ocean Front Walk. Rolly swung the car into a small side street and parked. We jumped out and ran a block to a busy boardwalk that paralleled a wide sandy beach and a moonlit sea. From the moment we stepped into the flow of strangers, we got swept up into a crazy costumed swirl of painted faces and half-naked skaters. Clowns on stilts juggled stars. This circus was pure oxygen. I felt more alive than I had all evening. We drama kids might be freaks in Bakersfield, but here's where freakdom was born.

"Quick!" I said. "We gotta find the Gas House!"

Big Daddy Nord was the owner of the Gas House. King of the Beats. We'd seen his picture in the newspaper: six feet eight, 400 pounds, dark beard, wearing a captain's hat. One newspaper article called his Gas House, "The West Coast wailing wall of the dispossessed."

"There it is!" Mary Ellen jabbed me.

It was a big building with four huge square pillars. As we got close, I saw faces in the shadows and the glow of cigarettes. Loud heartbeat music poured out of the entrance.

A cute guy in a black turtleneck blew a jet of sweet-smelling smoke and held out his wrinkled cigarette to me. It was such an unsanitary gesture. Then I realized it was marijuana. The real stuff that we'd heard about.

Mary Ellen grabbed the joint from the guy and inhaled deep, just like the people around us were doing. They spoke through constricted throats, holding in the smoke. Rolly inhaled and passed it to me. I tried a tepid inhale and choked. That got some laughs—not the nice kind.

"We're looking for Big Daddy Nord," I said, trying to speed things up.

"Call me Harbinger, sweet angel," said the cute guy. He gestured to the entrance.

We paid the small fee and got a dark-green GH stamped on our hands. The music was a chest hammer. A long-haired girl on the stage sang in a gravelly voice. She moved like an angry toy. The crowd was jumping to her song.

"Janis!" they screamed.

A young beauty in a loose-knit dress stroked Rolly's crotch and swept him off. She shoved her naked leg between his legs as they danced. He raised his comic eyebrows at us over her shoulder.

Mary Ellen pointed to the massive back of a man. Big Daddy Nord. He loomed over everyone. Welcoming, hugging, handshaking, like it was a profession. He took my hand in his big paw and grinned through his black beard. His eyes were dreamy. Then he focused on something over my head.

I turned and saw this tall skinny guy in a red sweater, brighter than my formal. Holy shit. It was Mort Sahl, the funniest comedian on the planet. I had all this guy's albums. I knew his routines by heart. Mort smiled at me. That famous grin.

"It's Crimson Sally, right?" said Mort.

I was anybody he wanted me to be.

"Yeah," I said. "The Purple Onion. Good times, Mort."

An exhalation of larky girls surrounded him with their autograph books and shoved me out of his limelight.

I dragged on offered reefers. The airborne Gas House dope hit me like a soft cloud. I kissed my green stamped-inked hand. My passport. This is where life had been keeping itself! In a grand old coffeehouse by the sea. I was home. I was never going home. I inhaled the arsenal of total abandon. The hammerhead beat of the band and Janis's vortex high notes. Dancing flesh bathed in a staccato light show.

I lost Rolly and Mary Ellen in the crowd, but it didn't matter. I loved every sweaty, pudgy, skinny, long-haired face around me. I think I kissed someone.

Then, across the room, I saw him. I saw *him*! At the edge of the crowd. Dressed in a rumpled light-blue tux. Running. Like him. Like us. Like we used to.

"Willard! Willard!" I screamed.

Couldn't he hear me? I pushed through the thick tide of weed-smelling bodies. I thrashed past elbows, arms, and legs. Breaststroked wildly through blinding, colored lights. I ended up against a solid wall of Day-Glo posters, turning just as Willard disappeared into a horizon of conga dancers.

"Willard!" I started to follow, but my legs got tangled and I fell.

"Hey. What's your problem?" Mary Ellen pulled me up. "You look freaky."

"It was him," I said.

Rolly rushed to my side.

"I saw Willard!" I said.

"Hey," said Rolly. "Let's find you a quiet place."

They helped me upstairs out of the crowd and into a big moldy office. Rolly shut the door. The music still came through.

My high dissolved into tears. I cried. Cried like I hadn't been able to. God, I missed him.

Mary Ellen held me. "Remember," she said. "You weren't totally in love with him."

"Shut up, Mar," said Rolly. "Cry it all out, kiddo. He was a great guy. I miss him too."

"You hardly knew him," said Mary Ellen.

"Will you shut the fuck up!" said Rolly.

I sobbed. "Leave me alone!"

I don't know how long I cried. I looked up into the face of a dead clock. It said seven.

"What time is it?" I said.

Mary Ellen held up her gold graduation watch.

"It's one," she said. "Wow, it's the next day."

"Holy shit!" I dried my eyes on the formal. "I'm supposed to be home by now!"

A big man opened the door, filling the frame. No mistake who that was.

"Mr. Nord," said Mary Ellen. "May we use your phone? We got a parental crisis here."

"Happens all the time," he said. "If it's long distance, make it short."

Mary Ellen threw Big Daddy Nord a kiss. He grinned, grabbed a plastic bag of weed from his desk drawer and ambled out.

I picked up the phone, heard the dial tone, and hung up.

"What the hell am I going to say?" I said.

"The old shuffle game," said Mary Ellen. "Tell them we partied late and you're sleeping over at my house and you'll be home in the morning. Hang up fast before they ask any questions."

Advice from an obvious veteran.

I picked up the phone again. Mary Ellen dialed for me.

"Is that you?" It was Daddy's voice. Not his kind, sweet, patient voice. What I heard was exhaustion. "Your mother's pretty upset."

We both knew that was an understatement. What had Mother's panic done to him? What would she do to me? I felt like I was dissolving into the black mouthpiece.

"It's just one," I said. "That's when you said to be home."

"No," he said. "It's one-thirty."

Shit. Mary Ellen's new watch was a half-hour off. Typical!

"I'm sorry, Daddy. Mary Ellen's watch must be slow. But don't worry," I said quickly, "I'm safe and still partying at her house. Just a girls' impromptu slumber party. I'll be home in the morning. You only graduate once. Right? I gotta go."

Bang. I hung up.

Oh, shit. I'd never lied to Daddy. Mother, sure, but not Daddy.

"Think he bought it?" said Mary Ellen.

"How the hell should I know?" I said.

Of course, he hadn't bought it. I'd never spoken to him like that before. I pictured Mother pacing in panic, looking at her watch, the two of them wearing a groove in the beige wall-to-wall. It wasn't hard to imagine the horror that awaited my return. Daddy on the porch. Me getting out of the car as the sun came up.

"You're home," he would say, as if he'd been holding his breath. Relief. I could count on his relief. He would hug his short-sleeved warmth into me. I would smell his long night, his sour fear. What it had taken to keep Mother calm.

I was already ashamed of what I'd done to him. He'd always treated me like an adult, linked his arm in mine when we walked and talked together. He would do that, link arms, and we would face our house where Mother waited, stewed, roasted herself into full-blown vindictive distress. Seeing my sorry face would boil her right over the top.

Nord's musty office came back into focus.

Mary Ellen was calling her mother to deliver a quick lie. I envied her stress-free maneuvering. She was back with her Mom, now that her crazy Dad had moved out.

When she was done, she handed Rolly the phone for a check-in with his folks.

"Hey," said Rolly. "I'm a guy. I don't do check-ins. Let's boogie!"

"I want to go home," I said.

"I'm hungry," said Rolly.

He held the keys, so we followed him downstairs from Nord's office. I sat without appetite while Rolly and Mary Ellen scarfed down big plates of salty fries and sloppy burgers, drank beers and talked to everyone.

I was so down from my high. But everything was still unreal. Janis capped the night with an orgy of manic high notes, and shared her whiskey. Big Daddy Nord pressed our shoulders warm with his big hands and told us to stay real. All I could do was sit and rumble with a panic that I could barely control.

Finally, the three of us stumbled out of the Gas House into the early blue light of morning. The sea breeze smelled so fresh after all that pot. Walking to the car along the boardwalk, piles of party litter actually looked decorative.

Wasted and happy, Rolly climbed into the back seat, curled up, and fell asleep. Mary Ellen climbed in next to him, reached into his pocket, and handed me the keys.

"I don't know how to get home," I said.

"You'll figure it out," she said. "You got a license."

She collapsed on Rolly's butt and closed her eyes.

I rolled the windows down so that the cool morning air would keep me awake. My sense of direction, like everything else about me, was pure instinct. I drove slowly, feeling my way. Looking for street signs, I wound us through bigger, wider streets, with rock music blaring on the radio. Bleary-eyed, I almost missed the sign for the freeway entrance that took us in the opposite direction of the Beats' siren song.

It seemed like forever and no time at all. The highway got brighter as the day opened up. Once we reached the silent foothills of the Tehachapis, I drove a little faster toward home. I held the wheel tight, feeling the terror subside. Something shifted as I drove. A calmness that seemed to come out of nowhere, like another kind of high in the mountain air.

Sure, I owed Mother and Daddy an apology. But it wasn't going to come out of fear. Something else had been set in motion. I felt like I'd already left home. And that the descent back into the dry San Joaquin Valley was temporary.

Tonight, I'd been initiated into one of the many new worlds that was waiting for me. This was my journey. And it had finally, finally begun.

IN GRATITUDE

To my editors Suzy Vitello, Andrew Durkin. To the Pinewood Table participants and Flight of the Mind friends. In gratitude for all the advice, solicited and unsolicited from friends and family in the US and Mexico who read the book in the early stages. And to those who blurbed the book.

And in case I've forgotten to mention someone, please know that I am eternally grateful to all of you who have helped escort this book to the finish line.

ABOUT THE AUTHOR

Jan Baross is an award-winning author, filmmaker, screenwriter, and artist. She lives in Oregon with her dog, Sophy. This is her third novel. Visit her online at janbaross.com.

MORE BOOKS BY JAN BAROSS ON AMAZON AND KINDLE

Jose Builds a Woman

First Place for Fiction, National Kay Snow Awards.
Magical realism in the tradition of Márquez.
"What a romp! Let Baross take you on a wild ride through an extravagantly carnal Mexico of the imagination!"
—Ursula Le Guin (*Left Hand of Darkness*)

Sylvia the 100-Year-Old Assassin

"This is a tender look at what it means to be old, full of bad ideas and good intentions. The women's dangerous quest is a non-stop tumble of fun. Also, slightly scary."
—Joanna Rose (*A Small Crowd of Strangers*)

In Living Color

"This book of poems is dedicated to family—not a family expressing love by silent revery, but by wild truth."
—Kim Stafford, former Poet Laureate of Oregon

Ms. Baross Goes to Paris

Illustrated memoir and travel guide. Baross's culinary adventures in Paris with Henry Miller's ex-chef.
"A charming witty book with sophisticated illustrations."
—Lynn Jeffres (*Dali Code*)

Ms. Baross Goes to Cuba

Illustrated memoir and travel guide.
"The author's experiences living with a middle-class Cuban family and witnessing their daily struggle to survive."
—Aysha Griffin (*Leonardo's Revenge*)

Ms. Baross Goes to Mexico, San Miguel de Allende
Illustrated memoir and travel guide.
"Baross's experiences in this most magical of places with well-crafted sketches."
—Mark Saunders (*Nobody Knows the Spanish I Speak*)

Old Hong Kong
"This photographic book is a brilliant visual and historical artifact of Hong Kong's past."
—Z. Franks (photographer/writer)

Oregon In Bed on A Sunday Morning
"Intimate portraits of people in their bedrooms on Sunday morning."
—Robert Aughenbaugh (photographer/author)

www.ingramcontent.com/pod-product-compliance
Ingram Content Group UK Ltd.
Pitfield, Milton Keynes, MK11 3LW, UK
UKHW062258290726
14090UKWH00017B/773